a real enuff love

A Novella

Michelle Davis-Newell

SCRIBERITE
PUBLISHING LLC

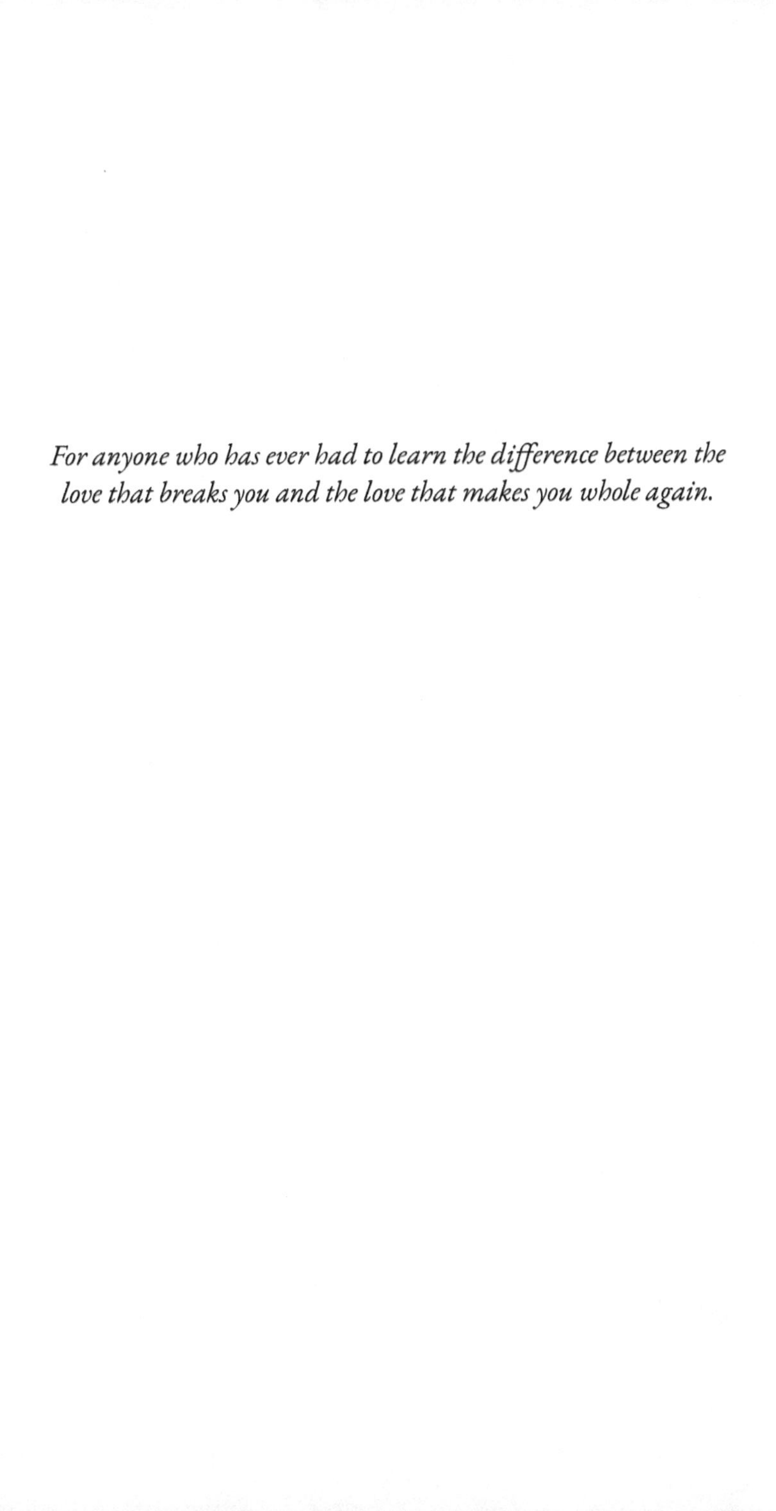

For anyone who has ever had to learn the difference between the love that breaks you and the love that makes you whole again.

Every love has a soundtrack. This one's Raina and Ezra's. Play it… and you'll hear them in every note.

🎧 Listen to the "A Real Enuff Love" Soundtrack

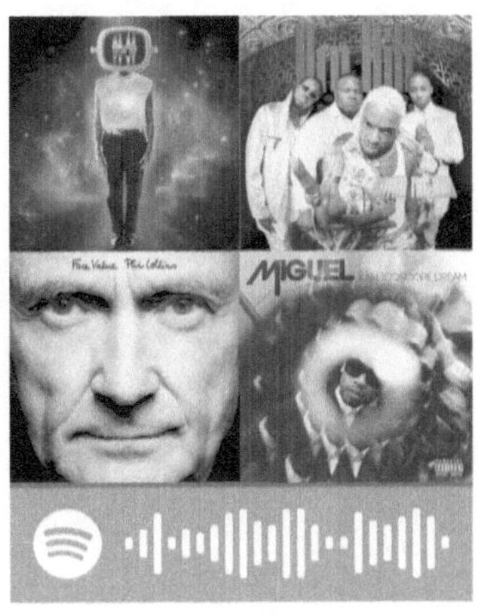

chapter
one

"I **NEED** some time to think about where I wanna be right now."

That was the last thing he said to Raina Simone Parker before she disconnected the call in his face and contemplated every decision she'd made in life up to that point.

Not him using that tired-ass Donnell Jones line.

The worst thing about it? She wasn't really into him.

Franklin Dean had pursued her with the fervor of a man hell-bent on delivering both joy and orgasms daily.

"Girl, if you let me," he'd crooned on their third date. "I'll keep a smile on your face and an arch in your back."

He failed at both. Spectacularly.

"Asshole," was all she could muster, the word a tired puff of air. She didn't even have the energy to conjure all the names she wanted to call him.

Scrub.

Emotionally stunted shit-tard.

Orgasm deadbeat—'cause he was hardly there and made no contributions when he was.

That breakup call was three weeks ago today, and she hadn't put pen to paper since.

Why was she having any kind of emotional reaction to someone she barely liked?

Because it was the first time she'd taken a chance on a relationship after her failed marriage six years ago, that's why.

Terrance Whitmore was no husband of the year, but at least he knew how to make her scream his name from one end of the house to the next. A small consolation prize for the heartbreak hell he left her to burn in, but at least she got something out of the deal.

Franklin couldn't come close. So why did she even bother?

She slow-dragged into the bathroom, then stared in the mirror after washing her face. Her deep brown, almond-shaped eyes, usually sharp and discerning, were clouded with a lingering frustration. A faint pillow crease was stamped across her cheek, a temporary mark on her warm, caramel skin. Her hair, a wild crown of soft natural curls, was flattened on one side from sleep.

She traced the shape of her full lips, lips that had kissed a few frogs and still never got her Prince Charming, and wondered if she looked as crazy as she felt.

Raina didn't ask for much. At thirty-four, she had built a solid life for herself. A successful career as a headhunter for a major pharmaceutical company had afforded her a swanky condo she loved. She had no children, no nieces or nephews because she was an only child, and no pets—just a quiet, organized world she had curated by herself, for herself.

Her philosophy on dating at one point had been simple: if a man showed up and put in the real, honest-to-God effort, that was a good start. They could build from there.

But after Terrance, she realized how little value she was putting on her time. And her heart.

She had listened to her best friend, Zaria Dean, about her lack of a dating life after divorce, and she had convinced her to give Franklin a chance four months ago.

"Sis, you've been single for six years. Your lil battery-powered bae can only do so much. Don't you miss being held?"

And that's what Franklin did well. His cuddle game was strong. His culinary skills were otherworldly, and he cleaned up after himself like an old-school maid.

But Zaria's cousin was petty. If Raina didn't overly compliment his cooking or pat him on the head for making the bed extra cute, he threw a temper-tantrum only rivaled by a toddler.

Thank God for that battery-powered bae Zaria teased her about. If it weren't for that, Franklin would've been disqualified after his second burnout at the o-**limp**-ics. Because "cooking and clean'ting" were about the only things he had stamina for...

"Girl, why did you break up with my cousin?"

Zaria's high-pitched 7a.m. squeal was not on Raina's bingo card today. She sashayed in on a wave of expensive perfume, unapologetic confidence, and energy that put the Duracell bunny to shame.

She was in full Cookie mode this morning—a body-hugging blouse tucked into tight jeans, nails manicured into sharp, blood-red and white claws, and a designer bag slung over her shoulder. Her hair was a sleek, jet-black bob that framed a face with sharp cheekbones and black-lined eyes that could spot a lie from a hundred paces away. And on her petite, five-foot-two frame, it all somehow worked.

Raina blinked at her friend's early-morning vitality, yawning deeply as she followed her to the kitchen.

Zaria set a cupholder with two large foam cups on the counter. "Franklin called me this morning saying you didn't even fight for him."

Raina barked a laugh with a shake of her head, taking one of the cups and sipping the hot liquid.

Strong ass coffee. A necessity on Monday mornings.

"Zaria, your cousin needs a psychiatrist, not a woman."

"I'm just saying, Ray." Her eyes narrowed, and her tone shifted, becoming more analytical. Raina recognized her friend's "Employee Relations Investigator" voice—the one she used right before she was about to dismantle someone's weak argument in a workplace dispute. "I know Franklin got his ways, but he's a good catch."

"And I'm throwing his ass back in the sea so somebody else can catch him."

Raina led Zaria to the small, solid pine breakfast nook.

"Franklin has great qualities," Raina explained. "But dude came at me with some mess about needing space. Fuck outta here with that lame-ass "I just wanna see if she feelin' me" trope. I wrote that damn book, remember?"

Zaria face-palmed with a slow shake of her head.

"Oh lord, no he didn't go there," she groaned, then gave Raina a guilty look. "I think I may have given him that idea."

"What?"

"When he said you were emotionally aloof, I made the comment, 'some people don't miss the water until the well runs dry...'"

Raina laughed out loud.

"And this fool thought if he pretended to want space, I'd what? Throw myself at his feet and beg him to stay?"

"He said he's been trying to call and apologize—"

"And texting, and showing up at my house. My neighbor Ms. Oleta had to threaten to put a spell on him to make him stop."

Zaria laughed so hard she snorted. "I'm sorry, sis. I really thought y'all could make a cute couple."

Raina smiled at her friend. "I love you, girl. But I'm good. I told you that. I don't need a man in my life—"

"Just in your bed, right?" Zaria's side-eye matched her dry tone.

"Well..." She couldn't deny this truth. "Listen, after Terrance put me through emotional purgatory, I hung up the towel on love and anything even close to it. Hanging out, having good sex, and maybe a few bars of conversation is all I need."

Zaria looked at her dubiously. "Girl. Who do you think you're talking to? First of all, you are the queen of romance. Your entire life is built on writing about love."

"Part-time queen," Raina corrected. "And that's just it. I *write* about romance. Doesn't mean I need or want it."

"Tell that lie to your lil fan club. 'Cause I know the real Raina Simone. And she loves falling in love like the rest of us."

"Ohhhhh!" Raina exclaimed with a knowing smile. "I see what this is. You've been hit by the love bug! Jason finally put it on ya!"

The twinkle in Zaria's eye gave her away as she tried to shield her smile with a sip of her coffee.

Raina leaned over and hugged her. "Listen, homie. I'm so happy for you and Jason, and I wish y'all the bestest and gushiest romance imaginable. As for me? I don't need, want, or desire anything resembling love right now."

Zaria's twinkle dimmed into something soft for her friend. "Damn. Terrance really did a job on you, didn't he?"

Raina shrugged. "You were there." She perked up. "But, look on the bright side. I lost seventy-six pounds after he crushed my spirit, and six years later I'm still down to my high school weight. So, silver linings, right?"

Zaria's eyes burned with anger. "If you had let me go over to his house like I wanted, I could've taken care of Mr. T and his ugly-ass woman right then and there."

Raina laughed—a genuine, stomach-clenching chortle. "Love you, bestie."

"I love you, too, sis. And I'll kill a knee-grow dead for you." She paused. "Well, except for my cousin. That's blood, you know how it is."

"Listen," Raina said, more serious now. "I do appreciate your fierce love. But right now, I need to focus on getting this book done. I only have ten months left on my leave from the real gig, and if I don't turn this writing slump around, I'll be going back to work."

"Yeah, I know how much you hate the thought of that. That was brave, taking a year off to focus on your writing."

Raina sighed, a deep, weary sound. "Brave or stupid, I'm not sure yet." She swirled the coffee in her cup. "Ten books, Z. Ten books I've poured my soul into. Nine of them I published myself, scrambling for every reader. And, finally, finally, I get a traditional publishing deal for the last one, it generates five figures, and my agent is breathing down my neck for the next manuscript."

Zaria's smile was supportive. "Nice problem to have, though."

Raina nodded. "You're right. Because, this is it. My chance to finally do this for real, you know? The one thing I love doing more than anything in the world."

"Writing's the only thing I've seen give you pure joy," Zaria acknowledged as she stood up. "Well, don't let me keep you from your money, Stink."

Raina followed her to the door. Before she walked out, Zaria turned to her, a teasing smirk tugging at her lips.

"Hey, maybe you can write the perfect love story and fall in love as your own character."

Raina laughed. "First of all, it ain't the story that makes you fall in love. It's the person in the story."

"Well hell, write *him*," she said as she toodle-ooed down the stairs.

Raina chuckled, shaking her head as she closed and locked the door.

Zaria's last words echoed in her mind like a ridiculous, teasing dare.

"Well hell, write *him*."

"Girl, you are nuts," she said out loud in the empty apartment. "That kind of stuff only works in the movies."

She headed to her home office and opened her laptop, determined to prove her friend—and her own frustrating writer's block—wrong.

She could do this, dammit!

She stared at the blinking cursor on the blank page for thirty solid minutes.

Nothing sparked.

The story that had been flowing in her head weeks ago was gone, the well completely dry.

"What the hell is wrong with you, Raina Simone?" she seethed, slamming the laptop shut with a satisfying click as the blinking cursor mocked her.

Her love story was dead.

Fine. Let it be dead—just like her love life.

She pushed away from her desk, not toward the kitchen for a sensible breakfast, but straight to the freezer. If she couldn't write a love story, she could at least eat her feelings about its demise. She grabbed the pint of chocolate chip cookie dough ice cream, the condensation cold against her warm, frustrated hands.

And if a little sugar-fueled chaos came from it?

Well, she was long overdue for some of that, too. Maybe then she'd be able to write a half-decent outline.

chapter
two

THE JULY AIR was thick outside, still smelling faintly of firecrackers and grilled food from the holiday weekend.

By afternoon, Raina still couldn't concentrate. The words, the settings, even the plot refused to materialize.

Defeated, she moved to her oversized couch with pillows that could double as a twin-size mattress and scrolled through her phone. She may as well delete some old photos she thought as she came across a few that served no purpose other than to eat up gigabytes.

And of course, her ex-husband took up the most space. Pics from when they dated, videos and photos of the day he proposed, and even more memories of their life together.

It was time for a delete party. She selected and discarded each and every one of those moments that had her smiling on the outside, but crumbling internally.

There must have been thousands. Why hadn't she deleted them sooner?

She had to admit—they had looked good together back then.

It had started, of all places, at a gym—a place she'd avoided her whole life. But after a stark warning from her doctor about her weight, which had climbed to 256 pounds, and a pre-diabetes scare, she'd reluctantly signed up.

She spent the first few weeks hiding in the back of classes, trying to shrink herself, her movements always a step behind everyone else's.

And then he saw her—his eyes fixed, making her seem like the only woman in a space filled with slimmer, more coordinated women.

Terrance loved thick women, he'd claimed, his eyes roaming over her curves with an appreciation that wasn't a measurement, but a confirmation. He wasn't just her trainer; he became her biggest cheerleader.

Their dating life was a whirlwind of experiences designed to make her the center of his universe. He took her to fancy restaurants, bought her clothes that celebrated her shape, and praised the creativity she had always been proud of.

But it was the dancing that truly broke down her walls. He knew how much she hated the gym, and one afternoon, after hearing her talk about her parents and the old-school R&B they'd play and dance to, he found the spark. "You love to dance, right?" he'd asked. "That's how we'll do it. No more treadmills."

He taught her Chicago-style Stepping in his living room on Sunday afternoons, the smooth, soulful music a backdrop to their own intimate rhythm. His hands were firm and patient on her waist as he guided her through the steps, their bodies moving together in a fluid conversation.

Soon, their weekly ritual moved beyond his apartment. They started going out to Steppers' sets, gliding across packed, dimly lit dance floors all over the city. For the first time, Raina felt not just desired, but graceful, a part of a beautiful, magnetic culture, with Terrance as her perfect, attentive partner.

And that's why she'd married him. The sex was admittedly spectacular—in a league of its own. But it was more than that. He was smart, funny, and he fueled her imagination and passion.

He had been her miracle.

Which made his betrayal an even crueler twist of the knife.

Where Raina considered her looks average, she had a penchant for pretty-boys. And the gods broke the mold with Terrance.

He was the quintessential man—six-foot-five with the kind of lean, sculpted frame that made dress shirts look sinful and sweatpants slutty. His skin was a warm, golden-brown, like the sun fell in love and kissed him daily. He had full, sensual lips. Long, beautiful eyelashes. His hair was always cut low in a tight, wavy fade that gleamed under light like velvet.

He laughed low and slow, like he was the keeper of secrets. He held eye contact long enough to make her stomach flip. And he touched the small of her back—gently—when he passed, even if there was plenty of room.

Terrance was fine-fine—the kind of fine that made strangers do double takes and women want to risk it all.

And he knew it. His charisma was his chosen weapon, and he wielded it like a man born to break hearts, only to offer to help pick up the pieces—knowing he would drop them again later.

Bastard.

It was his mama and daddy's fault, really, 'cause who told them to make something that damn dangerous and let it roam the earth? Stalking, preying, shattering souls.

Raina zoomed in on the photo that restarted her achy-breaky heart. It was taken the year before they got divorced.

~

August 2018.

Hawaii was beautiful, like she imagined it would be.

The resort looked like something out of a dream—tucked between emerald cliffs and sapphire waves, with private ocean-front bungalows nestled right at the water's edge. It was a place couples came to fall in love again.

And for the first couple of days, that's what Raina thought they were doing. Falling in love again, reconnecting what had been disjointed because of Terrance's infidelity.

They made love with the windows open and the ocean as their soundtrack. She'd watched him nap with one hand over his stomach, his golden skin glowing under the ceiling fan, and thought, this is what marching toward forever feels like.

But, damned if forever didn't have an expiration date.

It started with the shift in his energy. The sudden need for "space" after the third day—who the hell comes to a secluded island with his wife looking for "space?" The secretive texting while he said he was checking work emails. The way he kept his phone turned facedown on every surface.

Then she saw it.

A message notification had chimed while he was in the shower. He left the phone facedown on the nightstand, a silent black rectangle full of secrets she'd been trying to ignore. A little voice, the one that had been screaming at her for months, whispered, "Just look."

For once, she listened. She reached out, her hand steady despite the tremor in her soul, and flipped the phone over. An unrecognizable name—"Jade"—and a line that hit like a slap:

"Wish I was there with you instead of her."

Raina stared at the screen, the sound of rushing water and distant waves mixing into a low hum that drowned out the thrumming of her heartbeat. Her stomach twisted, her vision blurred—not with tears, but with a searing anger that threatened to burn a hole through the wall.

When he walked in from his shower, towel low on his hips, with that same smug smile he always wore when he thought she was watching, she blew a kiss at him, plastering the biggest grin she could muster. She'd seen this play out too many times over the two years of their marriage and the three years they dated. She had the apology script memorized.

*Raina said nothing about the message. She hadn't asked who Jade was. But she **had** made a decision.*

She put on her "gonna make you scream my name" playlist. The first song out of the gate was "Residuals" by Chris Brown.

She slipped out of the sheer robe, slowly and deliberately, the way he liked. She climbed on top of him, and kissed him like she was trying to remember what it was like to trust him.

She slid down his body, smirking at his involuntary gasp when she gripped his dick. She took him in her mouth and worked him with a cold, practiced efficiency. Her tongue, her hands—it was all a deliberate, punishing rhythm designed for one purpose: his undoing.

His eyes rolled, his hands grabbed the sheets, his voice cracked her name like a gospel choir...

You scream my name, but you give them my time, *she thought with bitter control as she moved faster, then slowed, then picked up the pace again.*

She worked him until he came and cried out, trembling uncontrollably.

Before he could recover, she quickly straddled him.

She rode that man like she was carving closure into his skin with every thrust.

As the drumbeat from Phil Collins' "In The Air Tonight" slammed through the room, she picked up the speed, clenching him with a grip that made him come undone.

After he climaxed a second time, and as she came, the tears she'd been holding back finally fell.

"Damn, baby ... I missed this," he murmured, breathless as she lay next to him. "You still cry when it's that good, huh?"

She nodded against his neck.

"He thinks I'm crying from this," she thought to herself. "He has no idea."

Those tears were reserved for the part of her that had wanted to believe in him. For the years she knew she'd wasted. For the pieces of herself she gave to a man who couldn't be faithful.

She recalled the very words she'd given to the protagonist in one of her stories: "When a man cheats the first time, you're a victim. If he continues to cheat and you stay, you're a participant."

She turned her back and curled into his side, letting him spoon her like nothing had changed. Like she didn't have exit plans already forming in her mind.

She'd finish the trip. Drink the champagne. Pose for the damn couple's photoshoot.

But when they got home?

She was gonna burn this love story down.

The memory faded, leaving the phantom scent of coconut oil and betrayal.

Raina had never been able to forgive ... or forget. Her paradise had been turned into hell, and the aftermath left her shattered. She'd divorced him a year later, after packing up and moving in temporarily with her parents.

Zaria brought her back from the edge of depression, but only after she brought Zaria back from the edge of going to jail.

She had shown up at Raina's parents' house with a gasoline can and a prayer candle when they found out Terrance had moved "Jade" into the house after Raina left.

"What are you doing?" Raina squeaked when she opened the trunk of the car.

Zaria had pure revenge in her eyes.

"It'll be a li'l fire, Ray," she protested with feigned innocence. "Not even a full burn. Just enough to smoke them out and tag their ankles with this baseball bat."

Raina had laughed. Then she cried. Then she hardened.

But six years later? She was still dealing with the aftereffects.

"Why does this shit still hurt?" She cast the words into the ether.

She grabbed her journal. With frustrated annoyance, she wrote,

> Dear future husband—wait, scratch that. Dear imaginary man with sense, stamina and no damn trauma—here's what I need. I only want to get my back blown out occasionally, have meals prepared for me that are so good, it's like having sex, and have a great conversation about anything and nothing. I don't need love—that shit's for the birds. Just a strong back, amazing stroke game and an ability to throw down in the kitchen. That's all a sista needs. If you're out there, I'll leave the light on for ya. 'Cause Zaria's right ... my toys can only do so much.

She set her pen down with a wry chuckle, then shook her head as she closed the journal.

"This is all a huge waste of time," she sighed, then closed her laptop as well.

There were no words today. She flicked off the light in her living room and lay on the couch. Within a few minutes, she was sound asleep.

chapter
three

RAINA WOKE UP BREATHLESS, one hand gripping the couch's throw cover, the other clenched between her thighs like she was trying to hold herself together. Her body trembled —not from an actual climax, because technically, she hadn't fully gotten there, but from the impact of the dream—which still lingered, deep and unfinished, long after her eyes adjusted to the room.

She looked at her phone. It was 2:37a.m.

She couldn't see her dream man's face, but she remembered the weight of his body, the deep, smoky timber of his voice, the way his hands curved under her thighs like they belonged there.

The things he'd done to her body?

Good God.

His voice had slid down her spine like silk, commanding in the most earnest way. He said her name as if she were adored. His mouth had moved over her skin as if he were committing it to memory. And his hands ... those gentle, powerful hands ...

Raina whimpered.

She threw the cover back and padded barefoot down the hall. The July heat still lingered in her bedroom, the ceiling fan creating a gentle breeze. She reached into the top drawer of her nightstand and pulled out the one thing that hadn't failed her in six years.

But tonight, the battery-powered bae didn't do the trick.

She tried.

She let it hum—hell, she even cranked it to the highest setting —pressing it to the aching throb between her thighs, letting her imagination take her back to the dream. But it wasn't the same. Her body clenched, teased, trembled—but it never tipped.

Eventually she came, barely, but it was mechanical. Hollow.

Like eating a slice of moist red velvet cake with no flavor.

Frustrated and sticky with sweat, she gave up.

Back in the living room, she slumped onto the couch, defeated. Was there anything in her life that wasn't a complete and utter disappointment right now? The men were a joke. Her creativity was ghosting her. And now, even her trusty vibrator had betrayed her.

But as she stewed in her frustration, Zaria's words echoed in her mind—that ridiculous, teasing dare.

"Well hell, write *him*."

A humorless laugh escaped her lips.

Write the perfect man? For herself?

The idea alone made a familiar knot tighten in her stomach. The risk of it. The inevitable disappointment.

No. She couldn't.

But for Savannah? Her protagonist, who was stuck behind a wall of words that wouldn't flow?

The thought was a loophole. She could pour all the impossible standards and secret, irrational fetishes into a man on a page, one meant for someone else. She could be the architect of a perfect love without having to risk her own heart.

As soon as her decision settled, the knot in her stomach dissolved. Her shoulders, tense for weeks, relaxed.

Yes. This was it. This felt right.

A new energy buzzed through her. This wasn't work anymore; it was an exercise. A purge.

She opened her laptop to a fresh blank document. She pulled up her "Writing Vibes" playlist on Spotify, and the smooth, sensual notes of Miguel's "Adorn" filled the room. She put the song on repeat, then cranked the volume to the max.

She went to the kitchen and poured a full glass of red wine, downing it quickly. Then another. By the time she sat back down, the wine and the music had created a perfect, hazy bubble of creative freedom.

Fueled by dissatisfaction, frustration and two more big gulps of Merlot, her fingers finally hovered over the keyboard.

She started typing—not a story—but a blueprint.

CHARACTER: SAVANNAH'S PERFECT MAN

He doesn't walk into the room.

He appears.

Like he'd always been meant to be there.

She started with the basics—his frame.

His height—a strong six-foot-two, tall enough that standing beside him was like finding shelter, a frame that rendered her own five-foot-seven diminutive in comparison. His weight—thick and powerful, all dense muscle, nothing bulky or overdone.

Then came the details.

The slope of his jawline. The warmth of his skin—deep, rich, golden-bronze, like molasses poured slowly from the jar. A smoothness that begged to be touched ... and indulged.

She gave him a medium crown of soft coils, thick and wild like the sky before a summer storm. Not a single strand was tamed, yet it all made sense—as if the chaos was intentional. Regal, radiant, and unapologetically free.

His eyebrows were full, a little unruly at the edges, like they refused to be boxed in. His lashes were longer than any man deserved to have, framing the most elegant light brown eyes that were completely knowing. Like they could peer into her soul and tell her entire story.

Not like any man she'd ever been with—Terrance, Franklin, what's-his-name from freshman year in college—who only ever seemed to see their own reflection. No, these were eyes that whispered, "I got you" before a woman even asked for help.

She gave him lips that were a direct invitation. Full, plush, and soft, they parted just enough to hint at the warmth within. The lower lip was especially generous, with a supple, velvety texture that was designed to be tested by teeth and tongue. They were lips that made a promise—a silent, sensual vow of what they could do in the dark.

She gave him a voice that vibrated low and curled around her protagonist's name like poetry. She wrote that when he called out to Savannah, it made the woman's thighs clench.

Raina had to cross her own legs on the couch, a surprised little laugh escaping her lips.

Down, girl, she thought. *He's for the book.*

And the hands ... good God, the hands. Big, warm, callused enough to know pleasure wasn't always gentle. Hands that looked like they'd been made to hold her hips—and heal her at the same time.

Oh, Savannah, you lucky girl, she thought with a wicked smile.

And as she wrote, the air in the condo changed.

A subtle breeze kissed the back of her neck, and she quivered, mistaking it for an effect of the wine.

The wine in her glass vibrated. The Bluetooth speaker, which she had powered off to concentrate, blinked once like it remembered something.

But Raina, lost in her writing, didn't notice. She was too far into the zone.

Sweating now. Breathless, as her fingers danced over the keys.

He was the kind of man you didn't only want—you needed him, even when you didn't want to.

Even if you didn't know it.

Especially if you didn't know it.

When she finally exhaled, she had no idea how much time had passed. Her nightshirt was damp with sweat, and her hands ached from typing. She pressed save just in case this was the beginning of something.

Or the end of her damn mind, because despite all the hours she wrote, she'd only completed one page.

But every word on it was about him.

Ezra.

No last name.

She closed the laptop in exhaustion. She needed air.

She stepped out onto her balcony, the late-night breeze a welcome sensation on her hot skin. The city was asleep, with the occasional car driving God knows where.

The stars dotting the sky appeared extra close tonight, their sparkle noticeably bright.

"Writing late tonight, huh?"

Raina jumped at the voice of her next-door neighbor, who was on the adjacent balcony, tending to a collection of strange, moon-colored flowers with a watering can.

"Ms. Oleta! You scared the daylights out of me."

The old woman chuckled, a low, gravelly sound. "Sorry, baby. The air just felt ... busy tonight. Thought I'd come out and check on my night-bloomers." She finished with a plant, her gaze landing on Raina with an unnerving perceptiveness.

"You put a whole lot of energy out into the world tonight."

Raina, still buzzed from the wine and the writing frenzy, just blinked at the odd phrasing. "Oh. Uh, thanks. I hope I didn't disturb you. Just trying to get some work done."

Ms. Oleta gave a slow, knowing grin. "That's what I mean. Be careful with that gift of yours, baby," she said, her voice dropping lower. "Your words ... they have a power you don't even realize."

Raina managed a weak smile, her mind a complete fog of exhaustion. Ms. Oleta's words sounded wise, she was sure, but trying to decipher another one of her spiritual proverbs right now felt like trying to solve a Rubik's Cube in the dark. She just didn't have the energy.

"Thank you, Ms. Oleta," she said, her voice heavy with a weariness that went bone-deep. "I appreciate that."

She excused herself politely, then headed back inside. She flopped down on the couch, leaned her head back, and fell fast asleep just as the sun started to peek over the horizon.

The house was quiet.

But in the dark room, the light flickered on, then off. Then on and off again.

And somewhere, in a space just outside of logic and on the other side of longing ...

Something breathed.

chapter
four

THE FIRST THING Raina noticed when she opened her eyes was the comfort, which was precisely the problem. The crisp coolness of her cotton sheets, the familiar weight of her duvet, the soft pillow cradling her head—it was all deeply, intimately wrong.

She gave a slow, disoriented blink, then another. Sunlight sliced through the blinds, painting stripes across the far wall. This was her bedroom. Not the plush, oversized couch where she had fallen asleep, laptop precariously balanced on the cushions beside her.

She bolted upright, the sudden movement sending a dull throb through her temples. "How the hell did I get in my bed?" she mumbled, her voice raspy with sleep. Her mind scrambled for a logical explanation.

Sleepwalking?

Had Zaria come over with the spare key and put her to bed?

No, none of that seemed right.

Her hand fumbled for the phone on her nightstand. The

screen glowed to life: 8:38a.m. She let out a low groan. So much for her morning workout.

She swung her legs over the side of the bed, planting her feet on the cool hardwood floor. A deep stretch pulled a satisfying crackle from her spine. The syrupy, stale taste of red wine coated her tongue, a grim reminder of her late-night creative frenzy.

Driven by a singular, urgent mission—coffee—she padded to the bathroom. She scrubbed away the evidence of her impromptu wine binge with a vengeance, the minty foam of the toothpaste a cool, sharp sensation on her tongue.

Splashing her face with cold water, she braced her hands on the cool marble of the vanity and stared at her reflection.

This was the face of a woman who had survived a messy divorce and rebuilt her life. It was supposed to be the face of a woman in control. Right now, she looked like someone who had jumped headfirst into a dream and hadn't quite woken up yet.

Still wrapped in the worn comfort of an old college t-shirt and plaid pajama shorts, she stepped out of her bedroom, ready for the familiar sight of her cozy condo.

But it wasn't the sight that hit her first. It was the smell.

Not her usual vanilla candles, but the rich, dark-roast aroma of freshly brewed coffee.

Coffee she hadn't made.

The usual comfortable silence of her home seemed different now.

Heavier.

Occupied.

She paused at the edge of the hallway, her body hesitating even as her mind screamed at her to see what was there. She took a single, careful step around the corner and froze, her bare feet cold against the hardwood floor.

There was a man on her couch.

He was just sitting there on the oversized cushions, a silhouette against the bright morning sun pouring through the window; a solid, breathing presence in a space that was supposed to be hers and hers alone.

The air in her lungs turned to ice. She couldn't move. Couldn't breathe. Her heart hammered a frantic, terrified rhythm against her ribs.

He looked up then, as if sensing her, and his movements were slow, deliberate. He blinked, his eyes adjusting to her standing in the shadows of the hall.

"Good morning, Raina Simone. I made you coffee."

The voice. It slid into the tense silence, a low, steady baritone that vibrated in the air between them. It was a voice she knew but had never heard. It greeted her like an old friend.

"Who the hell are you?" she managed, the words clawing their way out, a ragged whisper that was meant to be a threat.

He tilted his head, his expression one of genuine, furrowed confusion. "You should know," he said with a bewildering sincerity. "You brought me here."

Every survival instinct screamed at her to run. Her eyes scanned the room, cataloging potential weapons, possible shields. The heavy lamp on the end table. The fireplace poker.

She glanced at the keypad by the door; the small red light of her alarm system was still on—still armed.

How did he get in?

He rose to his full height, a slow, fluid movement, and the sheer, solid reality of him stole the air from her lungs. His presence seemed to displace the atmosphere in the room, shrinking the space around her, the temperature climbing a few suffocating degrees.

She scrambled backward, retreating until her back hit the old piano against the far wall—a beautiful, dusty inheritance from her grandmother that she never learned to play. She scurried behind the solid, heavy frame, finding some comfort in the only other thing in the room large enough to offer a shield.

The scream that had been building in her chest seemed performative a moment ago. Now, it was a necessity—the only logical response to an illogical reality. The sound that ripped from her throat wasn't a shriek. It was a guttural, animal roar of pure, system-shattering panic.

His hands flew up instantly, palms open and placating, his serene expression finally cracking with alarm. "Hey, hold on now—"

"The hell you mean, 'hold on'?" she screeched, fumbling behind her for anything solid as she stumbled against the piano bench. "Why are you in my house? Who are you?"

He took a careful step back, giving her ample space, his movements calm again. "My name is Ezra," he said, and his voice, so steady and familiar, was a balm against her panic, which only scared her more. "Please don't be afraid. I'm not here to hurt you."

Her logical mind—the part guided by fear—screamed that this was a grown-ass man who had somehow bypassed her alarm system.

A threat.

But another part of her, the writer, the creator, was paralyzed. That part recognized the impossibly familiar cadence of his speech. It recognized the proud slope of his jaw, the wild crown of his coils, the warmth of his golden-bronze skin, the knowing kindness in his eyes.

It recognized the name.

Ezra.

Don't you see the figment of your own damn imagination? A traitorous voice in her head whispered.

She refused to listen.

She chose logic.

She chose fear.

"Who are you? And how did you get in here?" Her hand subtly closed around a heavy ceramic coaster on the piano's edge. It wasn't much, but it was solid. "Did Zaria put you up to this? Is this one of those dumb-ass dating interventions?"

He smiled.

Lord, that smile.

For some reason, it made her feel even safer.

That was a problem. No woman should feel safe finding a grown-ass man she didn't invite into her house.

"No," he responded. "I wasn't sent here by your friend."

He held her gaze, and it was the kindness in his eyes—the "I got you" she had written for her character—that knocked the wind out of her.

He wasn't just a resemblance to her words. He was *the* blueprint. The unruly eyebrows, the impossible lashes ... it was all there.

Her heartbeat thundered in her ears. She recognized him.

"No," she said out loud, shaking her head.

Then she looked at him again.

"You're ... " she whispered, but couldn't bring herself to say the name.

His brows lifted slightly. "Ezra."

Raina's mouth went dry. Her knees buckled, and she stumbled past him to the couch, sinking onto the cushion, eyes wide.

"This ... this is not happening. I must still be asleep. Or drunk. Or losing my damn mind."

She looked at him again. "You're Savannah's man."

He looked confused. "Is that your name, too?"

Her eyes narrowed.

"That's from my book," she muttered. "You're ... you're supposed to be with Savannah, the character in my story. I haven't even written past the first page, but I had the whole thing planned. She was gonna be the woman you fell in love with." She caught herself. "I mean ... that Ezra was gonna fall in love with..."

She wiped her forehead, the turmoil reflected in her eyes.

"I woke up in your house," he gestured around him, "on your couch, with you. I don't know a Savannah." He paused, thoughtful. "But I know you."

Raina stared at him.

Hard.

"You're a character," she said flatly, convinced she had indeed lost her mind. "You're in my damn book. I *wrote* you."

He looked around the room casually, taking in her cozy chaos —the candles, the laptop, the empty wine bottle, the pillow dent where her head had been just hours before.

"Right now," he said, looking back at her, "I'm in your living room."

He smiled again.

"And unless you wrote this conversation too, I'd say things just got real... author."

chapter
five

RAINA PACED BACK and forth across the living room floor, her bare feet making soft, agitated whispers against the hardwood. She couldn't bring herself to look at him for more than a second at a time, but he was a silent, powerful gravity in the room, pulling at her attention even with her eyes averted.

Ezra. Her creation.

Here, in real time. In her living room.

He stood off to the side, leaning against the wall with his arms crossed over his chest, watching her with an unnerving curiosity. He wore a simple, heather-gray t-shirt and a pair of light gray joggers that hung loosely on his frame. The sheer normalcy of his clothes was the most insane part.

And beneath them ... the physique was exactly as she'd written it. Arms thick with muscle that promised a safe haven, a chest so broad it looked like a shield, and powerful thighs that even in the relaxed fit of his joggers, spoke of a strength she was suddenly very aware of.

She didn't know what was worse: that every primal instinct told her she should be terrified, yet she felt completely, illogically safe? Or that his gaze, which wasn't predatory or demanding, was wreaking havoc on her nerves with its patient earnestness—the same intensity she had written for him?

"I've got some questions for you," she challenged after a few minutes, stopping her pacing to mirror his stance, throwing her arms across her chest. "If you're from my book, prove it. What did I write?"

His smile was unhurried. He slowly, deliberately, presented himself—a single, elegant gesture from head to toe, as if to say, *All of this. You wrote all of this.*

She scoffed. "Oh, you got jokes. Why did I write you? And why didn't Savannah materialize?"

Let him try to rationalize that!

He pushed off the wall and stuffed his hands into the pockets of the gray sweats—making them hug his frame even tighter. He considered the floor for a long moment before his gaze—those knowing eyes—met hers again.

"I assume you wrote me, Raina Simone," he started, his voice soft but certain, "to be the man ... Savannah, is it? ... not only wants, but needs." He paused for a beat. "As for Savannah ... " He took a single, soft step closer. "You didn't bring her here ... because she ... and I'm only assuming, isn't what *you* need."

Smooth. That was smooth as hell. But she still wasn't buying it.

"None of this makes any sense. I should be calling the police, because how are you standing in my condo with the alarm still on?" The weight of the phone in her hand was suddenly a small, cold comfort.

"You could call the police," he said, unflinching. "But they won't see me. Only you can."

His calm certainty was infuriating. Before she could fire back a response, the sharp, sudden *BUZZ* of the intercom sliced through the tension. They both flinched.

Raina strode to the intercom, her mind racing as she pressed 'answer.' "Yes?"

"FedEx, ma'am," a polite voice chirped. "Package for Raina Parker, requires a signature."

A jolt of adrenaline shot through her as an idea formed, clear and purposeful.

"Come on up." She pressed the button to buzz the woman in and then disarmed the alarm system, her heart hammering against her ribs. This was it. The perfect, undeniable way to test his claim that only she could see him.

She turned to look at Ezra, and a slow, dangerous smirk touched her lips as she arched a single, challenging eyebrow. The look was a clear, unspoken declaration: *I'm about to call you on your bullshit, buddy.*

He had moved to stand in the middle of the living room, a silent, waiting statue, and the knowing, imposing grin he returned told her he knew exactly what she was about to do.

Raina swung the door open to a uniformed woman with a cheerful smile and an electronic tablet. "Hi, come on in while I grab my ID," she said, her voice a little too bright, a little too forced.

As she fumbled in her purse, she deliberately positioned herself to watch the delivery driver's eyes. The woman's gaze swept the room—and slid right over the six-foot-two man standing before her as if he were nothing more than an empty space between the couch and the bookshelf. Not a flicker of recognition, even when Ezra mockingly waved at her.

It was as if she were looking at nothing.

Raina's own hand trembled as she took the stylus to sign the tablet. Her mouth was dry. "Um…" she started, her voice strained. "This is going to sound completely off the wall, but … do you see anyone else in here with you and me right now?"

The woman's professional smile tightened, her own eyes darting around the room. She took a subtle, almost unconscious step back toward the open door. "No…?" she answered, her voice lilting up with caution. "Is someone else supposed to be here?"

A laugh bubbled out of Raina, high-pitched and unsteady. She waved a dismissive hand, glancing at Ezra, who was watching the exchange with that same exasperating, curious calm. "Nope! No one at all. Just … working on a little social experiment for a book," she lied.

"Oh. Okay." The woman's smile was gone, replaced by a strained look of someone who had just been handed a live snake. She dashed out the door after giving Raina her envelope.

The moment the lock clicked, sealing her back inside with this impossibility, Ezra's knowing grin returned, his voice soft and full of teasing victory.

"Satisfied, author?"

The air in the living room was suddenly thick with a heady, suffocating tension. Raina was reeling. After tossing her package on the end table, she found her spot on the couch again, clutching a throw pillow to her chest like a shield. Her mind was a whirlwind, trying to reconcile the impossible man across from her with the last dregs of logic she had left.

Ezra watched her with a deep, patient earnestness, as if he was waiting for her to catch up to a truth he already knew.

She fixed her eyes on the blank, eggshell wall on the other side of the room—a flat, boring, normal surface in a situation that was anything but. Her knuckles went ashen on the pillow she held like a lifeline.

Her voice was sharp when she spoke.

"You said something earlier. You said you 'know me.' Explain that. Now."

He moved a step toward the couch she was on. "May I sit?"

Her immediate, instinctive response was to yell "No!"

Instead, she pointed a rigid finger to the armchair across the room. "You can sit over there."

The distance was necessary. Safer.

Ezra sat in the chair, his movements fluid and easygoing. He inhaled deeply, as if gathering the facts. "Your name is Raina Simone Parker. You're an author, though you work for a pharmaceutical company. You don't hate that job, but you have no intention of ever going back. You're on a one-year leave to finish the manuscript your agent is waiting for so you can finally retire and write full-time."

Her eyes narrowed. "That's surface-level stuff. Zaria could have told you that."

He leaned forward, resting his elbows on his knees, his gaze so intense it was like he could see right through her. "Alright. I don't know everything yet. There are ... gaps. But I know you were born and raised on the south side of Chicago. I know you're an only child, but that Zaria is the sister you chose. I know your parents are retired and living their best life in Florida, and you miss them more than you let on."

He paused, his voice softening.

"And I know you once had a little green-and-yellow parakeet named Pepe, and that when he died, you were so heartbroken you swore you'd never get another pet again. And you haven't."

She flinched, a sharp, involuntary jerk of her shoulders. Her hand tightened on the pillow. That was impossible. No one knew about Pepe. Not even Zaria.

It was a silly, secret childhood grief she had buried decades ago, and he had just unearthed it with the casual precision of a surgeon.

"You've been burned in relationships so many times you've started to enjoy the taste of ash," he continued, his voice gentle but relentless. "Terrance was the one who lit the blaze that wiped out the forest, but you've been setting little fires ever since. You use men like Franklin as a smokescreen, a barrier to keep anyone from getting close enough to see the real you. That way, you don't have to risk getting burned again. It's like ... a controlled fire."

His words hit their mark, a volley of arrows finding their way through every crack in her armor. Her shoulders, once so rigid with defiance, melted. Her eyes misted, and this time, she didn't have the strength to look away from him.

"So ... do you know all my thoughts?"

He smiled, shaking his head. "No, dear. It's nothing like that. I can't read your thoughts—I only feel what you've left behind. Think of it like this: I'm a creation of your written words. So, I'm connected to the thoughts, desires, and pain that you've poured into your writing. And," he glanced toward her laptop, "you journal a lot."

After a few seconds of astonished quiet, her voice was soft as she asked, "How did you get here?"

He paused, his own eyes filled with sincerity. "I don't know. I just remember waking up on this couch, next to a beautiful woman. And, I didn't know at first how I knew her, but I knew I was connected to her."

His voice mellowed as he leaned back in the chair. "After a while, things started becoming clear to me. Like, this place. This is my ... my center. And, I don't think I can leave."

Her eyes narrowed with sudden recognition. "Wait—go back. You said I was on the couch when you appeared. But I woke up in my bed ... did you...?"

"I did," he said, matter-of-factly. "You were sleeping, sitting up. I knew that couldn't be comfortable. And you were snoring—loudly." He chuckled. "So, I carried you to your bed and put—"

That revelation alarmed her. Not only did he know the most intimate pieces of her—but now, he had been in her bedroom. The one place she held sacred.

Her stomach dropped, cold and nauseous.

And he had put her in bed.

That was her last thought—before everything short-circuited.

And just like that, her mind shut down. It was too much. The manifestation. The invisibility. The secrets he knew. And now, this—the image of this impossible man carrying her sleeping body into her bedroom.

Her hands went limp, the pillow slumping in her lap. She stared blankly at the wall, not seeing it. Her lips parted, but no sound came out. The edges of her vision blurred. The room, the man, the memory of Pepe—all of it melted into static.

She heard him call her name, but the sound was distant, like it was coming from the end of a long tunnel. She couldn't respond. Her brain, the one that built worlds from words, had finally found a truth too big to process. The logic board was fried. The system was overloaded.

There were no words left.

chapter
six

IT WASN'T the tenderness in his voice. It was the touch. The simple, warm weight of his hand on her bare forearm sent a jolt through her system so sharp it was like a defibrillator restarting her heart. He was kneeling in front of her, his face etched with a look of pure, unguarded worry.

"Please," he implored softly. "Say something."

His concern, the sincerity in his eyes—it made her heart do a stupid, traitorous flip. That intimacy, that vulnerability, was more terrifying than anything else.

She scrambled up from the couch, putting the entire width of the living room between them as a necessary buffer.

The silence that followed stretched, taut and fragile. Raina's mind, which had been a whirlwind of panic and denial, finally snagged on something else he'd said: he believed he was bound to her apartment.

The sheer insanity of that pushed past her doubts, replaced by a wave of indignant frustration.

"I need you to leave," she said, allowing no room for debate.

"I told you, I don't think I can," he defended, his brows furrowed in confusion.

"Oh no," she rebuffed, the sound sharp in the quiet room. "No, no, you absolutely *can* leave, because you're leaving right now. Get out of my house." She pointed a trembling finger at the front door, fueled by a desperate need to make her world make sense again.

To her surprise, Ezra didn't argue. He simply inclined his head, with an expression of calm curiosity. He pushed up from his knees and walked toward the door with a smooth, unnervingly graceful gait. Raina followed at a safe distance, her arms crossed tightly over her chest. Her heart hammered with a chaotic mix of wild hope that this would all be over and a frightening terror that it wouldn't.

He placed his hand on the doorknob, the simple metallic click echoing in the tense air. He turned it and pulled the door open.

The familiar carpeted hallway of her condo building was there, but so was something else, a thing she'd never seen before.

The open doorway was filled with a shimmering, almost invisible barrier. It seemed to vibrate with a low, silent energy, distorting the view beyond it like heat rising off summer asphalt. The air around it was charged, crackling with a power that made the hairs on Raina's arms stand on end.

"What the hell?" she muttered, her mouth and eyes widening in disbelief.

Ezra lifted his hand toward the opening. As his fingertips neared the threshold, the barrier solidified, glowing with a soft, golden light that repelled his hand with a gentle but absolute force.

He tried again, pushing this time, his muscles flexing with the effort. But his palm met the same invisible, unyielding wall. The longer he pushed, the more a faint, golden light seeped from his own skin, mirroring the glow of the barrier.

He couldn't pass.

Raina's curiosity was at war with her fear.

"What is that?"

She took a tentative step toward the open doorway. The instant her foot crossed the threshold, the shimmering wall of light vanished as if it had never been there. The normal, boring hallway greeted her.

She stepped fully out, then turned back, her heart pounding a frantic rhythm against her ribs. "Okay," she breathed, looking at Ezra. "Now you."

Ezra's hopeful expression returned. He took one step forward, but the barrier snapped back into existence with a faint, sharp hiss, blocking his path as completely as a bank vault door.

"No," Raina whispered, her writer's brain refusing to accept the impossible. She reached her own hand back through the open doorway, the air cool and empty where the barrier had been. "Take my hand," she commanded.

Her fingers were solid in his. He gripped them tightly. "Okay," he said, his voice full of a new resolve. "On three. One ... two ..."

On three, she pulled, trying to bring him through, and it was as if he hit a wall of solid energy. He was repelled again, stumbling back a step, but Raina, whose arm was still stretched across the threshold, felt nothing. No tingle, no force. Just the empty air of her hallway and the solid grip of his hand.

Her jaw was on the floor as she walked back in and closed the door, her hand resting on the cool wood. Neither of them spoke.

The part of her that built worlds with rules and logic was frantically trying to find an explanation.

A projection? Some kind of advanced hologram? A trick of the light?

But she had seen the way the air distorted, felt the crackle of energy, heard the sharp hiss. She had touched the space where it had been. There was no technology she knew of that could do that.

The impossible had just become undeniable.

But first, if she couldn't rationalize it away, she would have to break the logic.

A frantic energy of repudiation seized her. "Try the back door," she ordered, her voice thin. They rushed to the kitchen; he opened the door that led to the service stairs, only to be met by the same shimmering, golden wall.

"The windows!" she cried, pointing toward the living room. He cranked one open, and the sounds and smells of the city drifted in. A warm breeze washed over his skin, a welcome touch of the outside world.

But when he unlatched the screen and tried to put his hand through the open space, the invisible wall stopped him cold.

Raina thought about the balcony. It was her last, best hope. She slid the heavy glass door open, a wave of warm July air washing over them. "Try to step out," she commanded.

Ezra cautiously put one foot outside the door, his entire body stiff, and when the barrier did not appear, he and Raina both drew in a sharp, shocked breath. He turned to look at her, his face suddenly alight with a joy so pure and brilliant it was like watching the sun rise.

He stepped fully out onto the small concrete slab then. He was outside, under the open sky, the sun warming his skin. He closed his eyes, tilting his head back and taking a deep, calming breath.

For a single, breathtaking second, Raina's hope flared. It worked.

He took a confident step toward the railing, then another, but at the very edge of the balcony floor, he stopped abruptly, his body jolting as if he'd run into a solid wall of glass. The invisible leash held him fast.

He could barely lean over the rail, his hands gripping the metal, a look of profound longing on his face as he watched the world move below, while he was tethered to the building.

This was his limit.

Raina's heart plummeted. "You can't leave," she murmured as she stepped onto the patio, the final, paralyzing truth clicking into place.

Ezra turned from the railing, and she watched the brief, beautiful hope that had lit up his face moments before extinguish, leaving a quiet, soul-crushing sadness in its place.

He looked at her, and in his gaze, she saw the sincere grief of a man who had been given a glimpse of a world he could see and feel but never truly join.

A new, horrifying realization landed on her: He wasn't a person; he was a secret. Her secret. And looking at him now, she could see the weight of that secret was already becoming a burden.

They stepped back inside, the energy between them irrevocably shifted. The frantic denial had evaporated, leaving behind the heavy, suffocating truth of this new reality. Raina slumped onto the couch, burying her head in her hands.

He was here. He was her manifestation. And he was a prisoner in her home.

Oh my God, what have I done?

The thought wasn't a question; it was an accusation. She had been so consumed with her own pain she had inadvertently cast a desperate, selfish wish out into the ether.

And something had answered.

She hadn't just written a character; she had summoned a soul and trapped it.

Why was he here? Was he a punishment? A gift? And what was she supposed to do with him now?

These questions swirled as she looked up at him, at this beautiful, impossible problem standing in her living room. There was only one answer for now.

"Okay," she said, her voice heavy with resignation. "Okay. You can ... you can stay. For now."

Ezra simply nodded, but his eyes were filled with a gratitude so sincere and gentle it made her chest ache.

She took a shaky breath, standing up to face him, then laid down ground rules like flimsy sandbags against a rising tide.

"Rule number one: You sleep in the guest room."

"Guest room," he repeated, his eyes twinkling. He gave her a playful point, followed by a soft click of his tongue—a gesture that was equal parts obedient and entirely too charming. "Got it."

"Rule number two," she continued, her voice gaining a little strength. "No walking around shirtless." She tried for stern, but it was difficult when her eyes kept betraying her by flicking toward the sculpted expanse of his chest, visible even through the fabric of his t-shirt.

A corner of his mouth ticked up. "Even if I'm hot?"

"Especially if you're hot," she deadpanned. "And rule number three: under no circumstances do you touch my bed. Don't even go near my room."

"Wouldn't dream of it," he said, but the teasing, challenging light in his eyes told her he had every intention of making *her* invite him into it.

She looked him dead in the eye, her last rule the most important. "And you stay out of my way. You don't touch me, you don't interrupt my work. We are roommates. That's it. This is just until I can figure this out."

He held her gaze, his expression softening again. "I understand, Raina." He turned toward the guest room, then paused, looking back at her with a new seriousness in his eyes. "I'll follow your rules. But I have one of my own."

She blinked, surprised. "You have a rule?"

"I do." His voice was low but firm. "I won't be a burden here. I'm not someone you have to take care of. I'll learn to do things. I will cook, I will clean ... I will pull my weight."

She was so taken aback she almost laughed. "You're a ... a figment of my imagination. You don't have to do chores."

A small, proud smile touched his lips, a look of pure dignity. "A man has his pride, Raina Simone," he said with a playful wink. "Even a made-up one."

He turned then and walked toward the guest room, leaving Raina alone, completely disarmed by the unexpected depth of his character.

Her gaze landed on the empty wine bottle on the coffee table. She glanced at the clock on the wall. It wasn't even two in the afternoon. She wondered if it was too early to start on another.

And so began the new normal. The first few days were a quiet, awkward dance. Raina would work in her office, the door often closed, hyper-aware of every soft footstep in the hallway, every clink of a glass from the kitchen.

But slowly, his presence began to feel less like an invasion and more like a hum in the background of her life. A constant, buzzing question mark.

Where had he come from? How did he know regular, normal things? Was he a spirit? A dream? She had a thousand questions, and he had zero answers.

And without answers, all she had were the rules. The flimsy, ridiculous rules she had set, which began to bend, then break, not with malice, but with an innocent logic.

The first time, she walked in her kitchen to find him shirtless, sweat glistening on his shoulders, a dishrag slung over one. He'd been cleaning with a focus she hadn't seen since her grandmother used to prep for Easter dinner.

He just looked at her, pointed at the thermostat, and said, "It's seventy-six degrees in here, Raina Simone."

She had no argument. All she could do was retreat, her cheeks burning—and not from the temperature in the house.

The rule he broke most hilariously, however, involved her pink plush robe. She walked into the kitchen to find him at the stove, flipping pancakes while blasting and singing "Beauty" by Dru Hill with the confidence of Sisqo himself.

He was wearing her robe—the hem of which barely grazed his mid-thigh—and her silk bonnet, which was fighting for its life, perched precariously on the edge of his crown of coils.

Raina froze in the doorway, clutching her coffee mug like it was a crucifix to ward off a very beautiful, six-foot-two Black apparition.

She immediately thought about the bedroom rule, then it dawned on her: she'd put those items in the laundry room for today's wash.

He didn't turn, but she knew he knew she was there. He let out an exaggerated, theatrical sigh. "You didn't write me no clothes, Raina Simone," he grumbled, before finally looking over his shoulder at her, mock accusation reflected in his eyes.

She laughed, despite herself. "Do you ... do you even know how ridiculous you look right now?"

Ezra flipped a pancake. "You said don't be shirtless. I improvised." He paused. "You also didn't write me no drawers."

She almost spat out her coffee. "So we need to take you shopping," she guffawed. "Let's jump online and take care of this expeditiously. 'Cause sir. Respectfully..." She looked him up and down, and they both laughed out loud.

He was a sponge, absorbing her world at a startling speed, his skills evolving alarmingly fast. He was fascinated with all things online, especially the YouTube tutorials he watched to learn how to cook Raina's favorite foods.

His first few tries, however, resulted in her replacing her entire cookware set after he burned the salmon and almost set fire to the kitchen. But he learned quickly, and soon his execution was flawless.

His curiosity was immeasurable. He'd spend hours on the balcony reading books on everything from literature to astronomy.

One of his favorite pastimes was scrolling through social media, which he found hilarious, and learning the latest dance challenges on TikTok, often borrowing her phone until the battery died.

Tired of sharing, she dug her old iPhone out of a junk drawer and set it up for him. "For social media," she'd said, trying to sound casual, but they both knew it was more than that. It was a lifeline—a private line connecting her world to his, for the inevitable moments she would have to be out in the real one.

Sometimes she caught him journaling in the guest room, writing like a man running out of time.

Her condo, once filled with a comfortable silence, was now alive with the sounds of his chosen love language: music. He was especially fond of nineties R&B.

And then there was the sexual tension, like a third roommate that had moved into the small apartment and didn't pay rent —a constant humming presence.

How could it not be?

She had literally created the perfect man of her dreams, and Ezra was every bit the devastating vision she had put on the page. It wasn't just the physical—the broad chest she wanted to lay her head on, the powerful arms she ached to have wrapped around her.

It was his entire essence, a magnetic pull that took every ounce of her self-control not to break her own rules and simply devour him.

It was in the way he'd accidentally brush against her in the narrow hallway, his arm solid and warm, sending a jolt through her whole body that left her short-circuiting. The way she'd catch him watching her, a look of tender curiosity on his face that made her forget how to breathe.

One evening, drawn from her office by a familiar beat, she found Ezra in the kitchen, a wooden spoon for a microphone, dancing. He was moving with a smooth, fluid grace to the sound of Jodeci's "Freek'n You."

He was lost in the music, completely unselfconscious, and as he turned and saw her watching, he didn't stop. He just broke out into that rare, dangerous smile and held out a hand as an invitation.

Raina stood frozen in the doorway, her heart thundering. She saw it all—the innocent rule-breaking, the joy in his learning, the unnerving intimacy of his journaling, the heat in his eyes, and the effortless swag in his movements.

She was supposed to be writing a love story for Savannah, but the perfect male lead was doing a teasing body roll by her refrigerator.

She shook her head and fled back to her office, closing the door hard. But it was too late. She could deny it all she wanted, but leaning against the door, with the bass vibrating through the floorboards, she knew the terrifying truth.

She was falling for him.

Hard.

chapter
seven

AFTER TWO WEEKS of this weird new reality, the outside world seemed like a distant rumor. Raina's apartment had become her entire universe, a cozy bubble sustained by a steady stream of delivery bags and boxes.

Everything was brought to her: food and groceries, clothes and accessories for Ezra. He had developed a fondness for ocean-scented colognes and fell in love with vanilla and shea butter body wash, a scent that now seemed to perfume the air as he used it daily.

Zaria, of course, clocked the change in her friend.

"You sound different," she said over FaceTime, sipping a smoothie.

"No, I don't," Raina lied. "I'm just focused. I've been writing a lot."

"Mmhmm." Zaria narrowed her investigator eyes. "Why you whispering?"

"I'm not."

"You are. Is someone there?"

Raina's silence was a confession.

Zaria's eyes went wide. "Bitch. *Biiiitch*! Who is it? You got a new man and ain't told me?"

"No!" Raina hissed, scrambling off the couch and retreating to the master bathroom, closing the door softly behind her. "I mean … kind of. It's complicated."

Zaria blinked. "Complicated how? Oooh! You dating a married man?"

Raina rolled her eyes. "No, nothing like that." She leaned her head against the cool tile of the bathroom wall, the phone feeling slippery in her sweaty palm.

Should I tell her? The thought was terrifying. *She'll think I've completely lost it. She'll try to have me committed.*

But the thought of lying to her was even worse.

"Look, Z, it's not a married man. It's … remember that night we were talking? And you said I should just 'write him?'"

"Raina, what are you talking about?" Zaria's voice was laced with genuine concern. "Did you meet someone online? Is he catfishing you?"

"No! It's … he's … I wrote *him*, Z," she whispered, the words sounding insane even to her own ears. "I think I wrote him into existence, and he's … he's here."

A long, dead silence stretched from the other end of the line. When Zaria finally spoke, her tone had shifted. "Okay. You haven't been sleeping, have you? Did you mix wine and your allergy medicine again?"

"Zaria, I'm serious!"

"I know you are, and that's what's scaring me," she countered, her voice firm. "Alright, that's it. I'm comin' over."

"No, Z, now's not a good time—"

"I'm not asking, I'm telling," Zaria cut her off. "I'm ten minutes away. I'm bringing coffee, 'cause you don't need na'an lick of alcohol. Do not move. We're going to figure this out."

The line went dead. Raina had a ten-minute ticking clock.

She burst out of the bathroom to find Ezra in the living room at the window, leaning forward with his knuckles braced on the deep wooden ledge, staring down at the world below.

"My best friend is on her way over," she said in a frantic whisper. "She can't see you. You have to be completely silent. Don't move anything. Don't breathe too loud. Just ... be invisible. More invisible than you already are!"

Ezra turned from the window, a small, knowing smile playing on his lips. "Forgetting the rules already, author?" he chuckled softly. "She can't see a ghost, Raina. But, as you wish. I will be still."

Ten minutes later, the buzzer rang. Zaria entered after Raina opened the door, her face a mask of concern, a cardboard tray with two coffees in her hands. She immediately walked through and scanned the apartment, her eyes lingering on the empty spaces as if searching for cracks in Raina's reality.

"Okay, talk to me," she said delicately, setting the coffees on the end table in the living room. "Where is this 'complicated' man?"

Raina's heart hammered. She took a deep breath and pointed to the armchair where Ezra was now sitting. "He's right there. His name is Ezra."

Zaria's face fell. She looked at the empty chair, then back at Raina, her expression softening with pity. "Oh, honey ..."

"No, I'm not crazy!" Raina insisted, her voice cracking. "He's here. I can prove it." She turned to Ezra. "Help me," she mouthed silently, a desperate plea.

Ezra nodded once, his eyes calm and reassuring. "I got you."

Raina took a steadying breath and turned back to her friend. "Okay, Z, I want you to try an experiment with me. Go stand over at the kitchen counter and face the backsplash. And I'm going to turn my back to you out here. We both have to be turned around for this to work."

Zaria looked skeptical but willing to play along for the sake of her friend's fragile state. With a dramatic sigh, she walked to the counter and turned her back to the living room. Raina, in turn, spun around to face the patio door, her own back now facing Zaria.

As they both got into position, Ezra rose silently from the armchair. He moved with that unnerving grace into the kitchen, positioning himself on the other side of the island, giving him a perfect, unobstructed view of Zaria's front and Raina's back. He leaned against the far counter, casual and observant.

Only Raina heard the even tone of his voice. "Okay. This is perfect," he called out, focusing on Zaria. "Tell her to hold up fingers, but don't say how many, or which hand."

Raina's own voice trembled. "Hold up some of your fingers, Z, but don't tell me which ones."

From across the room, Ezra relayed the information. "She's holding up her baby and index fingers on her left hand."

Raina repeated this to Zaria, whose shoulders tensed.

"Okayyy..." Zaria's voice was tight with suspicion.

Ezra spoke again. "Tell her to make a goofy face."

"Make a goofy face," Raina instructed.

Ezra chuckled as he relayed what he saw. "She's rolling her eyes."

"Stop rolling your eyes, Z. Come on, now."

Ezra laughed out loud. "Your friend is hilarious. She just stuck her tongue out and she's giving the middle finger."

"Okay, what are you, twelve?" Raina tried to suppress a smile. "Sticking out your tongue and giving me the finger?"

Raina could hear the frenzy in her friend's voice. "Okay, this is crazy. You must have a mirror over there or something! There is no way..."

"She's looking at you now," Ezra said, finding the whole exercise amusing.

"Turn back around, Z!" Raina commanded. "One more. I promise."

She waited a few seconds, then asked Ezra, "Did she turn around?"

He confirmed. Then, his voice lost its playful edge, becoming soft and serious. "Tell her to pick up that pen from the counter and a napkin. Tell her to write a secret she's never told you before."

Raina relayed the message.

"She's grabbing the pen," Ezra said. "She's writing something..."

He was silent for a beat, and then he said with confusion in his voice, "She wrote, 'I lost my virginity to Nate.'"

Raina's head snapped around as if pulled by a string, her jaw on the floor. "Nasty Nate?!" she shrieked, all the rules of the experiment forgotten. "You told me it was Malcolm Henderson in his dad's Buick! You let Nasty Nate from the corner store take your virginity?!"

Zaria froze completely, then she spun around, her eyes wide with unadulterated shock, the napkin clutched in her hand. Her gaze darted from Raina to the empty armchair and back again. Her entire worldview was visibly fracturing in real time.

"How?" she spluttered, her voice barely audible. "How did you do that?"

"It wasn't me," Raina said, gesturing to Ezra. "It was him. He's here, Z. I told you."

Zaria walked into the living room and sank onto the sofa, her legs giving out. She stared at the empty chair for a long, silent minute, processing the impossible. Finally, she looked at Raina, her expression a mixture of terror and awe.

"Okay," she breathed. "Okay ... what does he look like?"

A jolt of inspiration hit Raina. Words were failing her. But an image ... an image was proof. "Hold on."

She grabbed her laptop. She pulled up an AI character design tool she sometimes used for motivation, her fingers flying across the keyboard. She typed in the description she had written just weeks before.

"Okay ... generating an image," she narrated for Zaria. "A Black man, six-foot-two. Skin like ... like sunlit molasses." Her voice was a low, intense murmur. "A crown of soft, wild coils. Unruly eyebrows. And eyes ..." she paused, her own gaze flicking up to meet Ezra's for a split second, "... make the eyes kind." She let her fingers move, typing in the key phrases she knew by heart, the secret language of his creation.

She hit 'Enter.' The program whirred for a moment. Zaria leaned in, her breath held.

An image resolved on the screen.

It was him. Not a sketch, not an approximation. It was his face. The eyebrows, the impossible lashes, the perfectly shaped lips, the gentle eyes. It was Ezra, pixel-perfect and undeniable.

Raina turned the laptop around. Zaria stared at the screen, then at the empty chair where the man on the screen was supposedly sitting. Her jaw went slack, her mouth hanging slightly open as a choked gasp escaped.

"Oh my God." Zaria was dumbfounded, looking at her best friend with a new, profound understanding. "Ray ... what did you do?"

The hour that followed was a blur. Zaria, her initial shock giving way to a rapid-fire investigative fervor, paced the living room, peppering Ezra with questions that Raina had to interpret.

"So you just... woke up on her couch?" she'd ask the empty armchair, her eyes wide.

Raina would listen to Ezra's calm answer and repeat his response. "He says yes, that's what he remembers."

"Okay, but where were you before?"

"Tell her there was no before."

"He says there was no before," Raina relayed, the words sending a fresh shiver down her own spine.

It went on and on, Zaria trying to fit an impossible man into a logical box, until she finally sank onto the couch, completely overwhelmed.

By the time early evening had settled, Zaria squeezed Raina's hand one last time before getting ready to leave, her eyes still wide with a mixture of fear and fascinated awe. "Now that I know, sis, I'm nervous and relieved. This is wild, even for me. I need to get home and get ready for my date with Jason, but I will call and check on you." She paused and called out to the air, "Bye, Ezra. It was … something … meeting you."

The moment the lock clicked behind her, the adrenaline that had been holding Raina together dissolved. The relief was so sudden and overwhelming it was like a physical weight, making her knees weak. She sagged against the door, the silence of the apartment pressing in on her.

Her best friend knew her deepest, wildest, most impossible secret. And that, somehow, made it less overwhelming.

When she turned, Ezra was standing in the middle of the room, his expression soft and patient. He opened his arms in a silent, simple invitation of celebration.

And for the first time, she didn't think. She didn't rationalize or build a wall. She walked into his embrace without hesitation, as if pulled by a force she'd been fighting for weeks. His arms closed around her, a circle of warmth and strength.

It wasn't too tight or too loose; it was a perfect fit. Her own arms found their way around his neck, her face pressing into the solid wall of his chest, inhaling the scent of his shea butter body wash.

A deep sigh of contentment seemed to reverberate up from his core.

The intimacy of the vibration made her pull her head back to look up at him. His eyes, full of a raw, unguarded emotion she couldn't name, were already on her. Her gaze dropped to his mouth—that devastating invitation she had written about.

Lulled by a force she couldn't—or didn't want to—deny, she rose on her toes and kissed him.

It was soft at first, a tentative press of lips, a curiosity of exploration. He didn't respond; he just allowed it, as if giving her the space to probe.

She pulled back an inch, her breath catching as she scanned his face. His eyes were closed now, his long lashes stark against his skin. Then, as if he'd made a decision of his own, his lips captured hers.

This time, it was a collision of pent-up longing, a messy, beautiful claiming. His tongue traced the seam of her lips, and she gasped, granting him entry. It was a dance of recognition, of two souls speaking the same language. The world tilted, and the only thing holding her steady were the firm hands that had moved to cup her face.

When they pulled apart, his essence lingered on her tongue—a heady mix of desire and want—while the radiance of his body still warmed her skin.

"Okay… that kiss felt … real," she panted, her voice dry. Her eyes traveled down to his pants. "Is … is … everything … real?"

A slow, dangerous smirk bloomed on his face. "Is that a real question?"

Before she could answer, he scooped her into his arms with an ease that stole her breath. Two quick, purposeful strides and he was lowering her onto the couch, following her down, caging her in with his powerful frame.

"Can I kiss you again, Raina Simone?" he asked, his voice a low, husky rumble that vibrated through her entire body.

She couldn't form words. She just nodded, her eyes locked with his.

He lay on top of her, his weight a delicious pressure, and eased effortlessly between her legs. This kiss was deeper, slower, a thorough exploration that sent waves of heat pooling in her belly.

As his dick stiffened and pressed against her core—a burgeoning hardness meeting her softness—he let out a low, involuntary groan. A jolt of pure, unexpected pleasure shot through Raina's system, making her gasp against his lips and meet his pelvic pressure with an upward thrust of her own hips.

The grinding friction of their fully clothed bodies was a sweet, maddening torture. She felt herself spiraling, her body clenching, climbing toward a peak she was both chasing and terrified to reach.

"Wait," she gasped, reluctantly breaking away from his lips, her hands pressing against his chest. "We've ... we've gotta stop. I can't—"

Ezra stopped, pushing up off her and extending a hand to help her sit up. The passion in his eyes was still blazing, a testament to the control he was exerting.

She couldn't meet his gaze. She forced herself to look away, but her eyes snagged on the prominent bulge in his joggers, a clear, defiant flag of his desire. A fresh wave of heat washed over her.

"I'm—I'm going to bed," she stammered, scrambling off the couch and forcing herself to walk away before she gave in to the raging inferno. She tossed a weak, dismissive wave over her shoulder, her mind a blank slate except for a single, repeating thought: "Nope. Absolutely not. Chile, I cannot."

She heard his voice, soft and laced with a small, knowing smile, before she reached her bedroom door.

"Have a good night, author."

She closed the door behind her, leaning against it, her body still trembling.

She had just made out with a figment of her own imagination.

And it was more real than anything she had ever experienced in her life.

chapter
eight

THE MORNING after felt like a hangover without the alcohol. A raw, explosive tension buzzed just beneath Raina's skin, a dangerous heat that had everything to do with the man sleeping in her guest room.

She stood in the kitchen, staring at the coffeepot as if it held the answers to yesterday's beautiful, terrifying chaos. But the pot was silent. The man who made the coffee, however, was not.

Beside her usual mug, a yellow sticky note was waiting.

> *Didn't mean to start a fire you weren't ready for. Still hot if you want it. (The coffee, that is.) — E.*

A corner of her mouth almost ticked upward before she forced it down. She should've been annoyed at his presumption, at the sheer, audacious intimacy of the note. Instead, a treacherous warmth bloomed in her chest.

That was the real problem—her own body betraying her, responding to his attention and wit when her mind was screaming at her to keep her distance.

She grabbed the mug, the ceramic warm against her hands, and retreated to the balcony for a sliver of space that was usually her own, even if he could follow.

The city buzzed beneath her, a world away and blissfully normal. Must be nice, she thought, taking a deep gulp of the coffee. It was perfect, of course. Just the right amount of cream and sugar.

This feeling—this dangerous, hopeful warmth—was too familiar. It was the same intoxicating high she'd had with Terrance in the beginning, the one that made the eventual crash so catastrophic.

Her fear wasn't of Ezra. It was of this growing pull to him. It was the fear of standing at the edge of the same cliff and knowing, with every fiber of her being, that a fall would break her.

Damn, damn, damn.

Her phone buzzed, rescuing her from her thoughts.

Zaria's image lit up on FaceTime, and Raina winced.

Of course. It was an interrogation she knew was coming but wasn't ready for. Reluctantly, she accepted the video call.

"Girl." Zaria's face filled the screen, already sipping a vibrant green smoothie. "You look like somebody snatched you out of a dream and threw you into reality with no landing gear. What happened after I left yesterday?"

Raina blinked. "That's your hello?"

"I said hello when I said 'girl'. This is a new topic, which means new tea. So spill. What happened?" Her eyes narrowed.

Raina didn't answer. She just took another long, fortifying sip of the impossibly good coffee, letting the silence scream what she couldn't say.

"Oh, hell." Zaria leaned so close her face filled the entire screen. "Raina Simone Parker. Don't you dare tell me you climbed that fine-ass magic man like a tree."

"We only kissed," Raina admitted, her voice a low murmur.

Zaria's eyebrow shot up. "And?"

"And I almost humped his soul out through his sweatpants, okay?" she hissed. "That man ... that thing ... whatever he is, he is dangerously well-designed, if you know what I mean."

Zaria cackled so loudly a pigeon flew off a neighboring ledge. "Get it, girl! I knew it!"

Then her expression sobered. "Okay, for real, though. You look and sound wrecked. This is moving too fast. You need to get out of that apartment and get some perspective. Meet me at The Grind in thirty."

"Z..."

"Nope. Bestie's orders. You need a reality check. Thirty minutes, Ray." The line went dead.

A half-hour later, Raina slid into the booth across from Zaria, the bell on the coffee shop door chiming a cheerful, mocking tune. It was almost surreal to be outside, surrounded by the low chatter of normal people living normal lives that didn't involve magical boyfriends.

"Okay, spill it all," Zaria said, pushing a latte toward her. "'Cause you look like you've seen a ghost."

"Worse," Raina muttered into her cup. "I think I'm falling for one."

She recounted the entire electrifying encounter from last night, her voice laced with disbelief. "It just feels too real, Z. So real that it scares the hell out of me. And I can't tell what's genuine and what's just ... a symptom of my situation."

"Your situation being six years of unaddressed heartache and a bad case of being horny as hell for Casper the Fine-Ass Ghost?"

Raina winced. "You don't have to put it like that. But yes. Am I just projecting all that baggage onto this beautiful man who I literally created out of thin air?"

Zaria listened, nodding slowly, her expression thoughtful. "Look ... you haven't just been avoiding relationships, Ray. You've been actively sabotaging them, so now you don't know what's real anymore. You built this barrier around your heart after Terrance and refused to even open the gate." She took a sip of her smoothie. "You said from now on—and I quote—that all you wanted was someone to 'blow your back out every once in a while.'"

Raina dropped her head into her hands with a groan, her own words coming back to haunt her. "I sound so pathetic."

"You sound human," Zaria corrected with a gentle hand squeeze, then her eyes lit up with her familiar, problem-solving spark. "Okay. So you're in what we'll call a 'supernatural situa-tionship.' There's only one way to know for sure about what you're feeling. You've been in a perfect bubble with a perfect man for weeks. We need to pop that bubble for a night and see what happens."

She paused, deep in thought, before enthusiastically hitting the table. "I'm setting you up with a normal, non-magical dude."

Raina grumbled. "No, not that again—"

"If you sit across from a real, living man and you're still thinking about Ezra ... then you have your answer. It's about him. But if you get even a little spark, then maybe you're just ready to date again, for real."

Raina wanted to argue. Part of her knew it was a ridiculous plan. But the writer in her was desperate for a logical answer, no matter how absurd the experiment. Looking at her friend's determined face, she also knew it was a losing battle to protest.

She stared into her cup, watching the swirl of foam dissolve into the coffee.

Was she truly falling for Ezra?

What if this pull was just horniness dressed up in a beautiful body with a voice that made her knees weak?

She'd been inside with him for weeks, drowning in a fantasy that felt more real every day. The more she pushed him away, the more she wanted him. The avoidance wasn't a defense anymore; it had become its own kind of foreplay.

He was the ultimate forbidden fruit, living right there in her guest room, and every "no" she told herself just stretched the rubber band between them tighter. A part of her, a dangerous, reckless part, was dying to know what it would feel like when it finally snapped.

Maybe Zaria was right—maybe the only way to know if this feeling was real was to step outside of it. She had to know if the rubber band would finally snap from the strain, or if a single night of freedom was all it would take to make it go limp.

"I can't believe I'm saying this," she sighed, rubbing her temples. "But fine."

"Sis, worst-case scenario: you get a free dinner. Best case? You remember you're still alive and capable of real feelings with actual human beings."

~

When Raina walked back into the apartment, the silence was soft—a welcome reprieve from the noise of the city.

Funny ... that never bothered her before.

Ezra was on the patio, and the sight of him—sitting out there, looking at a world he couldn't touch—sent a complicated pang through her chest. At the sound of the lock clicking, his head turned. He met her gaze, then rose and slid the glass door open, stepping inside.

"Hey," he greeted with an easy smile.

"Hey," she managed, returning a weak smile of her own.

"How was it?" he asked, his eyes full of light. "Being out there?"

The simple question, the genuine curiosity, caused a bubble of guilt to settle in her gut. "It was ... nice," she said, tossing her bag on the couch. "It was good to get out."

He nodded, but his gaze was perceptive, his head cocking to the side. He watched her for a long moment, the silence stretching until it became a question in itself. "Why does it feel like there's more, Raina?"

Her stomach fluttered with nerves. She reminded herself: *He's not your man. He's a man you wrote. There's a difference.*

But she knew that was an oversimplification of this very complex situation.

"Zaria, she, uh ..." She tried to laugh it off, a brittle, awkward sound. "She has an idea."

Ezra's eyebrows arched with caution. "An idea about what?"

She took a breath and just ripped off the Band-Aid. "She wants to set me up on a blind date."

It wasn't a dramatic, theatrical reaction. It was quieter, and somehow, so much worse. The light in his eyes extinguished completely. His smile dissolved, leaving his face a blank, smooth mask. It was like watching a masterpiece revert to a blank canvas.

A thick, stunned silence filled the room. Then he turned and walked back to the patio door, his shoulders stiff as he shoved his hands into his pockets. He stared out at the city, his back to her. When he finally spoke, his voice was flat, devoid of the warmth it held just moments before. "And ... you agreed?"

"Well, I mean, I think it's a good idea," she stammered, hating how defensive she sounded. "Just to see if—"

"To see what?" he cut in, still not looking at her. "To see if a 'real' man feels better than a fake one?"

The words were a gut punch, brutally direct and laced with a pain she couldn't deny she'd caused.

But how? How is he ... evolving to feel this way?

They were not a couple—why was he having a reaction like a jealous, scorned lover?

"That's not what I was going to say."

"Tell me this, Raina," he challenged. "And be honest. Am I real to you?"

She opened her mouth, but nothing came out. After a few seconds, she found the words.

"Ezra, I can't lie to you. I ... I ... don't know what's real any more."

He turned his head to the wall, and the rigid line of his back nearly broke her. "Am I real to you?" he repeated, and it was no longer a simple question. It was a raw, aching demand, laced with a desperate frustration she could feel in her own bones.

Her head dropped, and her voice dipped. "No."

His head turned back to the patio door, processing her admission as he stared through the glass. The silence was heavy. He let out a long, slow breath, his shoulders slumping before he forced them straight again. Then he turned around with a polite, hollow smile plastered on his face.

"You know what?" he said, and his voice was so bright and forced it made her flinch. "Zaria's right. You deserve to have fun. You've been cooped up in here for weeks."

It was the most distancing thing he could have said. She was witnessing the shift in him in real time, and it was devastating, because it felt like he was building a wall between them. He walked over to her, and she thought—hoped—he might touch her, might kiss her like last night.

Instead, he stopped a full foot away, leaned in, and placed a chaste, gentle kiss on her cheek—a kiss that held a void.

"Enjoy your date, Raina," he said softly. "I hope he's everything you wrote me to be."

And then he walked into the guest room and closed the door, the soft click of the latch echoing in the enormous, suffocating silence of the apartment.

Raina stood frozen, her hand coming up to the cheek he'd just kissed. His words replayed in her head, like a devastating checkmate. He hadn't just given her permission; he had given her a standard to judge the rest of the world by.

And she knew, with a sudden, sickening certainty, it would be almost impossible for a real man to measure up.

Because she had written him to her standards of perfection.

chapter
nine

Ezra

EZRA LAY STARING at the whirring blades of the ceiling fan in the guest room, his hands laced behind his head, fingers pressing into his soft coils. He was still reeling—hard—from Raina's announcement.

A blind date.

The words themselves stung like a physical slap. He had no claim on her; he knew that. He knew she had a right to date; in fact, he understood her need to. But the thought of her with someone else...

A raw, nameless emotion clawed its way up his throat, feral and sharp.

But it was her answer to his question that had blown a dimension-sized hole through his entire being. He replayed it, a masochistic loop in his mind.

"Am I real to you?"

"No."

The denial hadn't been loud, but it had detonated in the quiet apartment, leaving a gaping wound where his heart should be.

Did he even have a heart?

It certainly felt like it was breaking. He was drowning in a storm of emotions he was only just learning the names for: a hot, searing jealousy; a profound, aching hurt; and a sense of powerlessness that was the cruelest torture of all.

He needed air. An escape from the walls that were both his sanctuary and his cage.

He swung his legs off the bed. The living room was quiet, but he could hear the faint spray of the shower from behind her bedroom door. The sound, so intimate and mundane, only twisted the knife deeper.

He strode to the patio door, sliding it open with more force than he intended. The cool air was a balm to his heated skin. He sank into one of the chairs, dropping his head into his hand, and then stared out at the city—a beautiful, glittering marvel full of wonders he could only ever watch from his gilded cage.

A half-hour later, the sliding of the patio door pulled him from his thoughts, the sight of Raina knocking the wind out of him. Every ounce of his anger, his frustration, it all just ... evaporated. He stood as she stepped out.

She was wearing a navy blue dress. The ribbed fabric clung to her curves, a second skin that moved with the subtle, confident sway of her hips. The neckline dipped low, revealing the smooth, warm expanse of her collarbone, a place he wanted to touch, to trace with his fingertips.

"I'm about to head out," she announced, uncertainty in her voice. "I just ... I wanted to make sure we were okay."

The word "we" settled in the space between them, precious and fragile. He swallowed past the lump in his throat and offered a supportive smile.

"We're good, Raina Simone," he said, his voice a little rough. He cleared his throat. "Go. Have fun."

"Are you sure?" she questioned. "You seemed a little upset before—"

"I was just having a moment," he smiled encouragingly. "I'm sure. Just, text me and let me know you made it there safely."

Her expression softened with relief. She took a step forward, hesitated, and then closed the distance between them, wrapping her arms around his waist.

It was unexpected. But it was everything.

He instinctively wrapped his own arms around her, pulling her close and burying his face in the crook of her neck, breathing in her scent—warm vanilla and something that was just purely, intoxicatingly her.

A few moments later, he was alone again, watching from the balcony as her car disappeared into the river of traffic. The warmth of her hug faded, leaving behind a sharp pang in the center of his chest.

He leaned on the railing, careful of the barrier, lost in thought as he watched the city move on.

"Must be weird," a low, gravelly voice said from the adjacent balcony. "Seeing the world you now belong to, but can't touch."

Ezra looked over, startled. On the adjacent patio stood an older woman with a vibrant purple head-wrap and kind, knowing eyes. Her skin was the color of warm, rich mahogany, and a thin, white cigarette rested between her fingers.

He assumed she was talking to herself—Raina had told him about the quirky next-door neighbor. He turned back to the view of the city, his own sorrow a heavy cloak.

"Don't worry, child," the woman spoke again, and this time there was no doubt. The words were not for the sky; they were for him as she met his gaze. "Your secret's safe with me. I've been seeing things that ain't quite there my whole life."

The world seemed to sway. Time slowed, the distant city sounds fading to a dull hum as Ezra turned to her fully. Every instinct in his brief, borrowed life screamed that this was impossible. He was a secret only one person could see.

Should he be afraid?

He scanned her face under the setting sun, truly seeing her for the first time. The intricate lines around her eyes, the relaxed set of her mouth, the wisp of silver smoke that curled from her lips.

She wasn't looking at the space where he stood; she was looking at *him*. Her eye contact was direct, steady, and full of a sympathy that comforted him.

No, she was definitely not someone he should fear.

"You ... you can see me?" he finally asked, his voice rough with disbelief, the words feeling foreign in his own mouth.

The woman took a long, slow drag from her cigarette, the smoke coiling around her head like a silver halo. She gave him a sad, wise smile. "Clear as day, honey. My name's Oleta."

It was as if a tightly wound spring deep inside his chest had finally been released. His entire body softened, the rigid lines of his posture melting away into a look of heartfelt relief. He gave her a small, watery smile of his own. "I'm Ezra."

She nodded, a softness in her eyes. "I know, baby."

Ezra took a step closer, his mind racing to catch up with this new, inconceivable reality. "But ... how can you see me ... talk to me?" he pressed, his voice full of a desperate need to understand. "Raina has been the only one—I'm invisible to everyone else."

Oleta took another thoughtful drag of her cigarette. "To most folks, you are," she said simply. "But in my family's lineage ... let's just say we see things. We feel things. The veil between worlds is a little thinner for us."

She studied him for a moment, her gaze seeming to see right through to the very soul of his creation. "And let me tell you something else I see. You ain't a ghost. A ghost is a soul with unfinished business, something left behind. You ..." she paused, her eyes kind, "... you're a soul that was called here on purpose."

Ezra stared, hanging on her every word. It wasn't just that she could see him; she *understood* him.

"In my family, we have a name for what you are. We call you a Kè-kama."

The words rolled off her tongue like the smoke from her cigarette.

"It means 'Heart's Echo.' A soul that wasn't born, but answered a call."

She smiled at the wonder in his eyes.

"You, my friend, are a Spirit of Longing. When a person, especially a creative soul like Raina, hurts so bad and for so long ... when they want something with every fiber of their being ... sometimes the universe can't help but listen. All that pain and hope gets tangled up, and it spills over, looking for a vessel."

Ezra's mind reeled.

A Heart's Echo.

It sounded both beautiful and profoundly sad.

"Does this happen often?" he asked, curious about his so-called origin story.

"Noooo," she shook her head. "It's as rare as a full moon during a winter solstice. I've only heard of it happening once, generations ago on my great-great grandmother's side."

He was unique.

He let this sit for a moment, the greatness too big to fathom.

Why him? Why Raina?

Why now?

"Am I real?" His voice dipped low, as if afraid of the answer.

Ms. Oleta gave a single nod, smiling as if she understood the "why" of his question. "Can she touch you?" When he affirmed, she continued. "Do you eat? Do you sleep? Do you feel?"

"Yes," he nodded, the single word full of a desperate certainty.

"Then you're real."

The confirmation, simple and logical, delighted and confused him.

"But ... if I am real ... why can't I leave? Why am I trapped here, in the apartment?"

Ms. Oleta took another long drag of her cigarette. "Because this is where she wrote the spell, honey. Every magic needs an anchor. A root. For a Golem, it's the clay it was made from. For a Heart's Echo ..."

She paused, letting the weight of her words settle in the space between them.

"It's the vessel that gave it form. You weren't born into the world; you were born onto a page, in that very house. The apartment isn't your cage, baby," her voice was a gentle, heart-breaking whisper. "It's your source."

"But *how*?" he managed to ask, his voice raspy. "How is any of this possible? And ... how did you know she ...?" He couldn't finish the word.

Created.

Oleta let out a warm, throaty chuckle. "These old walls are thin, baby. I hear things. A word here, a word there." She paused, taking a drag from her cigarette. "I felt the energy coming off this apartment in waves. And then, I saw you out here a few weeks ago. "

She tapped her temple with a long, frail finger. "It ain't hard to put two and two together when you know what you're looking for."

Another wave of relief washed over Ezra. For the first time, someone was offering information on who and what he was—an external validation Raina, who was just as in the dark as he, could never provide.

"I still had to do my research on this one, though," she admitted with a small, self-deprecating laugh. "Like I said, I've only *heard* stories about the Kè-kama. But the old tales all say the same thing."

Her voice dropped lower, more intimate as she leaned over the railing separating them.

"A soul as loud and as full of longing as Raina's ... she doesn't just write; she prays with ink." A knowing look crossed Ms. Oleta's face, and she shook her head slowly. "I tried to warn her once, you know. Tried to tell her about the power she puts behind her words."

She paused, taking another long, thoughtful drag from her cigarette.

"She believed in the *idea* of you so desperately, she opened a door between what's real and what's written."

Ezra's mind was racing, trying to grasp the sheer, terrifying scale of it. "A door—like a cosmic door?"

Ms. Oleta nodded, a small, sad smile on her lips. "You got it. And that child poured so much of her own spirit into the creation of you—all her needs, all her hurts, all her secret desires—that she created a vacuum on the other side of it. And the universe, honey, it abhors a vacuum. It had to send something back to fill that space."

She took one last look at him, her eyes filled with a deep, almost maternal understanding that settled his chaotic thoughts into a single, devastating truth.

"That something was you. You became a debt the universe had to pay."

Ezra exhaled, the words settling into his very core.

A debt to be paid. A prayer to be answered. A heart to be healed.

He looked out into the starry night as the moon finally made its appearance. He didn't know *how* to reach Raina—how to break through the fortress of pain she lived in. But now, for the first time, he knew *why* he had to try.

Because it all made sense now.

The strong pull toward her. The confusing storm of emotions she caused in him. This new understanding clarified everything, and he got lost in the thought of her.

To him, Raina was the most beautiful chapter in a book he thought he already knew by heart. He had been "written" with a knowledge of her, but this new reality of her—the one standing on the other side of his creation—was a stunning, breathtaking revelation.

He thought about the woman who had walked out of the apartment to go on a date with another man, and now he saw a universe of details about her he hadn't had the words for before.

Her face was heart-shaped, her skin—a deep, sun-warmed caramel —glowing with a warmth that the apartment's soft light seemed to adore. She'd sometimes put on makeup, but it was so masterfully subtle it served only to amplify what was already there.

A soft, smoky liner didn't change her eyes; it simply framed the story within them.

Those magnetic eyes ... they were the color of rich, dark earth, intelligent and deep, holding a universe of unspoken novels, heartache, and a defiant spark of mischief that was pure Raina.

And her lips. He knew them now. They were full and perfectly defined, sometimes with a soft, rosy-brown gloss that caught the light when she spoke.

These were the lips that had trembled when she finally kissed him. They were the home of her wit and her vulnerability, and the memory of their taste was a phantom presence on its own.

Her curls, long and elegant, were a testament to time and patience, cascading over her shoulders like lines of poetry.

But she was more than the sum of her parts. He saw the proud set of her shoulders, the way her hands moved when she was making a point.

He saw the beautiful woman who got flustered, who loved R&B, who could be brought to her knees by a memory, and whose heart was guarded by walls she had built brick by painful brick.

He beheld the goddess who had, in a moment of desperate creation, forged him from her own soul. She wasn't just his author. She was her own, entire story. And he wanted to read every single page.

He finally had names for the sharp, ugly feelings Raina's blind date had sparked in him.

Jealousy. Hurt.

But what was the name for this? This vast, growing, all-consuming ocean of feeling that had been his entire reality from the moment he first opened his eyes and saw her? It was more than a feeling; it was the very essence of him.

He was so lost in the revelation of her that he didn't realize he'd zoned out until Ms. Oleta spoke, her voice soft and knowing.

"She's something else, isn't she?" she said, watching the play of raw, unfiltered emotion on his face. "To inspire a love like that."

Ezra finally looked back at her, his own eyes wide and misty with the sheer, overwhelming scale of it all.

Love.

That was it.

He took a breath, the wonder of it settling in his chest.

"Ms. Oleta," he asked, his voice weighted with a beautiful helplessness. "What kind of love am I in?"

A single tear escaped the corner of her eye, and she smiled through it.

"The kind that rewrites the rules."

chapter
ten

LATER THAT NIGHT, Raina sat across from a man named Marcus at a stylish, low-lit seafood restaurant with a vibe that was wonderfully perfect. Zaria had outdone herself.

When she'd first arrived, he met her outside, a huge smile of recognition plastered on his face. She was struck by his sheer size—not just tall, but solid, with the bulky, powerful frame of a man who clearly spent time in the gym.

His dark gray slacks were perfectly fitted, and the white dress shirt he wore was stretched taut across a broad chest and toned arms. His locs, the color of dark chocolate, were twisted into neat, uniform ropes and gathered in a low ponytail that fell to the middle of his back.

His face was kind, his features well-defined, with a strong jaw and a smile that reached his eyes. They were a generous brown, and as he wrapped her in a friendly hug, they scanned her with an open, appreciative warmth that made her feel seen.

Within the first ten minutes, as they were settling in with their drinks, Zaria texted her.

For the next half hour, she honored that promise. She was completely engrossed. She'd put her phone away, determined to give this a real shot, for Zaria's sake if not her own. And he was refreshingly easy to talk to.

"So Zaria tells me you're a writer," he began, leaning forward with genuine interest. "She said you write romance. What do you love most about it?"

The question was simple, but it wasn't the usual "Oh, so you write those steamy books?" that she always got. It was insightful. She found herself opening up, talking about crafting worlds and the magic of a perfect "meet-cute."

"I get that," he said, nodding. "It's like restoring a vintage motorcycle for me." A twinkle appeared in his eye. "You find this beautiful, broken thing with a history, and you have to have the patience to put all the pieces back together just right until it hums like it's brand new."

His laugh was easy, and she found herself warming to him completely. He told her about a recent trip to Ghana, his voice full of passion, and then gushed about his ridiculously spoiled golden retriever with the kind of unabashed love that spoke volumes of his character.

The conversation flowed ... easy and engaging.

She was laughing, a real, from-the-belly laugh, and a small, forgotten part of her thought, *Oh. This is what a normal, good date is supposed to feel like.*

It was, by all accounts, a really good date.

Which is what made the soft buzz of her phone under the table feel like a delicious, guilty, and entirely inappropriate thrill. She tried to ignore it, telling herself to be present. But a minute later, it buzzed again, a quick, impatient follow-up.

That was Ezra. She didn't even need to look to know. No one else texted her like that—a rapid-fire succession of thoughts, as if this nonverbal way of talking was a magic trick he couldn't stop performing; each message about a tiny treasure he had just discovered and had to share with her instantly, before it lost its charm.

Her curiosity was a physical itch she had to scratch. Excusing herself to the restroom, Raina pulled out her phone the moment she was out of sight, half-expecting a stream of consciousness about the texture of the ceiling or the sound of the refrigerator humming.

Instead, what she saw made her breath catch.

EZRA

So. What's this guy like? Is he funny? Or dull as those old knives in your drawer? The suspense is killing me. 🪦

Or is he so boring you've faked your own death to escape? Blink twice if you need me to call Zaria and report you missing. 👀 👀

A smile touched her lips. The text wasn't about the world. It was all about *her*. The realization was a dizzying and deeply flattering wave. The most fascinating thing in the universe to him wasn't the universe itself; it was her.

She was glad—more like relieved—that he was no longer upset about her date. She typed quickly.

RAINA

I'm safe. 😌 He's actually nice. And interesting. Zaria did good. He works with her in HR. And he has the cutest dog.

EZRA

A dog ... okay, that doesn't sound bad. So, what did you order?

RAINA

He had the poached salmon. I got the sea bass. It's pretty tasty, I'm just not that hungry so I barely touched it.

She walked back to the table, a complicated, confusing jolt in her chest.

She had been laughing at Marcus' jokes. She was having a good time.

And yet, the secret world she shared with the man at home was a magnetic, irresistible force.

Just as she sat down, her phone buzzed again.

EZRA

POACHED salmon?! 😳💀 Raina!!! He don't even like you! 😒

She laughed out loud, a real, full-throated cackle. Marcus looked at her with a confused smile on his face. "Something funny?"

"Sorry," she said, covering her mouth. "Just remembered something my friend said. You were telling me about your lovely dog?"

Raina's heart stumbled, caught itself, and started doing a completely new rhythm. Ezra couldn't even see her. He was going off memory.

And his memory of her—of the moment before she left to go on a date with another man—felt more present than the handsome, charming gentleman sitting right in front of her.

She tried to focus on Marcus. He was great.

But the pull of Ezra was overwhelming.

"You seem a little distracted," he said, his smile still kind, but his eyes held a flicker of confusion.

"I'm sorry," she said, flipping her phone onto its face. "I'm here."

She was on a great date with a good man.

But all she could think about was going home.

A final text vibrated against the table. She flipped it over.

And that's when she knew. Zaria's experiment had worked, just not in the way she'd intended. It wasn't that other men were lacking. It was that they weren't *him*.

It wasn't lust. It wasn't loneliness or cabin fever. She just missed *him*. Her impossible, infuriating, beautiful magic man.

Real or not, at this moment, he was the only one she wanted to be with.

~

Raina walked into her condo, the door clicking shut behind her. Marcus was nice, and at any other time, he would have been worth a second date. But being with him was like eating a rice cake when her soul was starving for red velvet.

As she dropped her keys into the bowl by the door, a soft melody floated through the air—a smooth saxophone, warm and familiar.

Paul Hardcastle. "Lost In Space." One of her favorites.

She slowed her steps as she entered the living room, and the sight that greeted her made her stop dead in her tracks. Her hand flew to her chest in a gesture of pure shock.

Well, clutch my pearls, she thought, an audible gasp escaping her lips.

It wasn't just a few candles. It was a scene of such overwhelming, golden romance that she felt like she'd walked onto a movie set.

Dozens of candles flickered on every surface, their low, soft light turning her modest apartment into something sacred, almost holy.

Her dining table, usually a graveyard for unopened mail, had been transformed—a white tablecloth with matching napkins, a bottle of red wine sitting in the middle, wine glasses and covered plates set for two.

It was the most romantic thing she'd ever seen.

And then there was him.

Ezra stood by the table, wearing a simple black button-down, sleeves rolled to his forearms. The top two buttons were undone, a silent, devastating dare to her self-control. His jeans were tastefully fitted.

His coils were freshly fluffed, his expression soft and achingly hopeful. He looked like a promise she was terrified to believe in.

"Welcome home," he said, his voice a deep rumble.

Her throat tightened. "What is all this?"

"I wanted to make you a proper dinner," he smiled. "I thought you might want ... something more satisfying."

He gestured toward the table, and the scent finally registered —lemon-dill, garlic and butter. He'd made her favorite meal: pan-seared salmon.

"I know your date was nice, but you said you barely ate," he added, a teasing glint in his eye. "So I figured you might still be hungry."

God help her.

She didn't speak as she walked to the table and let him pull out her chair, his fingers brushing her shoulder in a way that was anything but accidental.

The meal was perfect. The wine was perfect. But the real intoxication wasn't the food or the drink. It was him. The way he looked at her when she talked, as if every word held weight. As if she were the only story he cared to read.

By the time dessert was served—a single, perfect chocolate-covered strawberry he fed to her with his fingers—she was breathless from nothing but his attention.

Then, Walter Beasley's "Nice and Easy" swelled on the speaker. Her eyes lit up in recognition.

Ezra stood and extended a hand. "Dance with me, Raina Simone."

"Oh no, I don't dance," she declined shyly.

He leaned in, his lips brushing her ear, sending a shiver down her spine. "You do," he whispered. "You just forgot. Step with me, baby."

Baby.

That one word was her undoing. Her hand slid into his, and he pulled her into the open space by the couch. His palm fit against the small of her back as if it was made to be there. They moved together—deliberate, fluid.

"How did you get so good at Stepping?" She was breathless, the moves coming back like muscle memory as she glided with him, stunned and impressed by his ability to lead.

"You told me it was one of your favorite things to do back in the day. So, I learned."

The song faded into another, more sensual groove. Gato Barbieri's "Europa" was sultry—almost sinful.

Their movements instantly slowed, Raina's body responding before her mind could catch up as their thighs brushed with an electric friction.

His hand slipped lower, bold now, possessive. His fingers flexed against the curve of her hip, pulling her flush against him. She gasped, pressing closer, her breasts brushing the hard wall of his chest as they moved in perfect rhythm.

Their bodies were saying something their mouths hadn't dared to yet.

As the music faded, he tilted her chin up with his thumb, his eyes molten with a searing, unrestrained passion. "I've been trying not to kiss you since you got back, Raina."

"Just do it," she whispered with a challenging lilt to her voice.

And so he did.

It was not soft. It was a collision. A hungry, desperate claiming. Mouths crashing, tongues sliding over each other's with a familiarity that defied logic.

She moaned into his mouth, her fingers fisting in the soft coils of his hair, pulling him in deeper. Her lips were swollen, her thighs trembling as the thickening ridge of his dick pressed against her pelvis, hard and insistent. Her dress slid off one shoulder, and he groaned at the sight of her skin, a low, guttural sound of a man at his breaking point.

"Tell me to stop," he breathed against her lips, his voice a raw plea.

"Don't you dare."

That was all it took. He swept her into his arms, like a man done waiting. She clung to him, dizzy with lust and something dangerously close to love.

He didn't take her to the couch.

He didn't take her to the guest room.

He carried her to the one place she'd forbidden him access: her bed.

The room glowed with golden, flickering streaks from the living room's candlelight. He laid her down gently, as if placing something sacred upon an altar. And then, he worshiped.

He unraveled the dress from her body with a slow, patient reverence, his eyes roaming over every inch of newly exposed skin as if committing it to memory.

When she was left in nothing but her black lace bra and panties, he paused, his breath catching in a soft, audible hitch. His gaze sent a wave of heat washing over her skin—she'd never felt more beautiful.

His fingers traced the delicate edge of her bra before finding the clasp at her back. A soft click, and it was gone. His hands, so big and warm, cupped her full breasts with an agonizing gentleness.

Then, he hooked his thumbs into the sides of her panties and slowly slid them down her hips, down her thighs, and off her feet.

She was bare for him now, completely open, and the look in his eyes was of pure awe.

His mouth explored her body like it were scripture he was learning by heart.

Gentle, reverent kisses along her collarbone.

Slow, open-mouthed licks down her sternum that left a trail of fire.

His lips planted soft, searing kisses across her stomach that made her writhe, her fingers fisting the sheets.

He raised her legs, draping them over his shoulders as he lay flat on his stomach and settled his face between her thighs.

She gasped when his tongue traced the slick folds of her pussy, a slow, deliberate line of heat that promised a deeper exploration.

A low, wet sound filled the space between them—subtle, intimate, and so obscenely erotic that she almost lost it right then and there.

He didn't have to search for the treasure. He found it, as if her body were a map he already knew. He swiped his tongue over her pearl—a lazy, decadent motion that made her entire body jolt.

Her moan was a husky, broken note, echoing in the quiet room.

He sucked her clit softly at first, then with a firm, rhythmic pressure that sent electric pulses ricocheting through her body.

Her eyes rolled, her back arching off the bed, instinctively chasing the pleasure.

He held her steady, his fingers pressing into her thighs, keeping her open for him, until she shattered with a sharp, sweet cry of his name.

"Where did you learn that?" she panted, her body still humming.

"I told you," he said, his eyes locked on hers, lips glistening. "I know you."

She pulled him up by the shoulders, tasting herself on his mouth as his clothes joined hers on the floor.

When he positioned himself above her, he paused.

Their bodies were touching everywhere but the place that mattered most.

Foreheads pressed together, eyes locked, their ragged breaths mingled.

For one long, suspended heartbeat, they just looked at each other—seeing, choosing.

And then, with a slow, deep slide, he entered her.

It felt like home—like a key finding its lock.

They moved together in perfect sync, as he softly whispered her name in her ear. In a moment of overwhelming ecstasy, her nails raked down the hard muscles of his back, and he answered by capturing her hands, lacing his fingers with hers and holding tight.

Every slow, deep thrust was a promise. Every searing kiss was an admission.

And then it happened. A subtle flutter that started not in her body, but in her mind, right between her eyebrows. A warmth spread from there, spiraling down through her chest, her belly, coiling tight in her core before it detonated.

"Ohhhhh shit, Ezra," she breathed, her voice a low, husky lilt.

It wasn't a scream; it was a surrender.

A slow wave of pleasure crashed over her, leaving her completely undone, shaking while silent tears tracked down her face.

Her release, so total and overwhelming, was all it took to pull him over the edge as her pussy gripped him tight.

He followed with a hard, shuddering climax, his own guttural groan muffled against her neck as he poured himself into her.

"Fuck!" he yelled out, writhing in pleasure as he pushed further into her, his arms wrapping around her and holding tight.

He pressed his forehead to hers, both of them unraveling in the same shared breath.

They lay there for a long moment, breathing each other in. Her skin still hummed from where his hands, mouth, and tongue had been, every nerve ending lit and alive.

Ezra pressed a slow kiss to her temple before rolling to his side, keeping her close in the curve of his body. His arm stayed draped over her waist, a quiet anchor.

Somewhere in the background, the next song in his playlist had started—Heatwave's "Sho'Nuff Must Be Love." The melody slid into the room, soft and sure, wrapping around them like a shared blanket.

Raina's chest tightened. He didn't say a word, but he didn't need to. The song was the confession. His truth.

She closed her eyes, letting the warmth of his body and the weight of that music sink deep into her bones. His breathing evened out against her back, steady and unhurried, as if he already knew neither of them was going anywhere tonight.

No one spoke. The candles still flickered in the next room, the song whispered, and in this moment, there was nothing to question.

Nothing except the fact that she had just crossed a line she could never uncross.

And somewhere deep down, she knew the words in that song were waiting to be said out loud.

chapter
eleven

THE MORNING SUN CAST LONG, lazy stripes across Raina's bedroom. She lay wrapped in her sheets, her body a warm, purring memory of the night before.

Ezra lay beside her, propped up on one elbow, his fingers gently tracing the length of her arm. It was a soft, domestic intimacy that was both brand new and as old as time itself.

"I have to ask," she murmured, her voice still thick with sleep. "The candles ... the wine ... the salmon. How did you pull all that off?"

A slow, tranquil smile spread across his face. "I had help."

"Help from who? Did I manifest a butler, too?" she teased.

He chuckled, the sound a low rumble in his chest. "Something like that. It was your neighbor."

Raina's eyes snapped open. "My neighbor? You mean Ms. Oleta?"

"That's the one," he said, his voice soft at first, then filling with excitement. "She can see me, Raina. We talked yesterday while you were out. She ... she helped me understand some things. About what I am. About how I ... came to be.”

Raina sat up, pulling the sheet with her to form a protective barrier.

“She’s a very wise, spiritually connected woman,” Ezra continued with awe.

Ms. Oleta. Of course, Raina mused to herself. *The woman who burned sage and strange-smelling incense and always seemed to know things no one had told her.*

She didn’t know whether to be annoyed or concerned, but she wasn’t totally surprised. It was another layer of impossibility stacked onto an already teetering pile. Her secret magic man’s presence was spreading outside their three-person knowledge group.

The thought was strange and deeply unsettling.

“So, what did she tell you?” she asked, her voice a hushed whisper. “What are you?”

Ezra’s expression was a mixture of amazement and joy as he sat up. “She has a name for it in her family’s tradition. A Kèkama,” he said, the word sounding both ancient and new on his tongue. “It means ‘Heart’s Echo.’ She said I was a soul that wasn’t born, but answered.”

Raina stared at him, the poetry of the phrase giving her goosebumps. “Answered what?”

He leaned closer, his eyes full of a reverence that was all for her. “Your call,” he replied. “It wasn’t just the words you wrote, Raina. It was the pain, the hope, the years of longing you poured into them.

Ms. Oleta said a soul as loud as yours can sometimes make the wall between worlds thin. She said that you poured so much of your own spirit into me, I became a debt the universe had to pay."

The sheer scale of it stole her breath. She shook her head in wonder. "So ... could I ... could I do this again? Any time?"

Ezra's smile was gentle as he wrapped her in his arms. "No, baby. According to her, it was a perfect storm of magic and need that can't be replicated. You didn't just write a character; you wrote a prayer. And I," he kissed her forehead, "am honored to be the miracle that answered."

Later that day, a comfortable, couple-like silence settled over the condo. Ezra was on the balcony, completely absorbed in her last published romance novel. From the kitchen, Raina watched him.

She saw him chuckle softly at a line of dialogue, then saw his thumb gently trace a paragraph, a look of profound empathy on his face.

He wasn't just reading her story; he was reading *her*.

It was in the midst of this quiet, intimate observation that he looked up from the page, his eyes finding hers through the glass.

"I love you, Raina Simone," he called out.

It wasn't a grand declaration. It was a simple statement of fact, a truth he seemed to have read on the page and was now confirming with his heart, as if her own words had just given him the language for his.

The plate slipped from her soapy hands, clattering loudly in the sink. Her heart seized, going into a full-blown panic.

As poetic as the moment was, it was a problem. A huge one.

Last night had been a sensual, erotic miracle.

His admission, however, felt like a promise. And promises were things that could be broken.

This is what real, normal couples do, she thought, a wave of nausea rolling through her. *But there is nothing normal about us.*

For six years, she had managed to avoid the pitfalls of love. She wanted to keep it that way. Because no matter the magic that brought this beautiful man into her life, she did not see love as a miracle; it was a liability. A commitment. A risk of emotional debt she had sworn she would never take on again.

And now here it was, sitting on her balcony, offering the very thing she was utterly terrified to accept, in a package she knew, deep down, might be too magical to last.

Love.

The word wasn't a comfort; it was an alarm bell. A threat. A promise of inevitable, soul-crushing pain.

Terrance had whispered it while texting his mistress. Franklin had whined it when he wanted her to soothe his ego.

In her experience, the word was a weapon, and hearing it now from Ezra's beautiful mouth was dangerous.

She knew he was neither of those men. In fact, he was like no man in this world. But the theme of heartbreak was universal.

What if he was temporary? A beautiful, borrowed dream that could vanish as quickly as it appeared? Ms. Oleta might have told him he was a Heart's Echo, but that didn't change the fundamental fact of what he wasn't: human.

This realization was the cold water that doused the warm embers of last night.

This wasn't just mind-blowing sex anymore. This was emotion. This was attachment to a man who could, for all she knew, dissolve like mist in the morning.

Believing him when he said "I love you" wasn't some small risk; it was a potential future of devastation. A danger she refused to sign up for again.

And just like that, the first brick of the fortress around her heart was laid to fortify the existing barrier.

She didn't say it back.

And he didn't repeat it.

A week passed in a tense, confusing truce. Raina treated Ezra with a careful, polite distance she hoped would cool the fire that had ignited between them.

It didn't work.

She threw herself into her writing, using Savannah's fictional world as a shield, but her own reality was a constant, simmering distraction.

Ezra didn't push; he respected her unspoken boundaries, but his very presence was a battle she was losing.

Every time he emerged from the bathroom after a shower, wrapped in nothing but a towel around his waist and smelling like shea butter, an intoxicating lure made her forget her own name.

Every time he caught her eye and gave her that soft, beautiful smile, her resolve would crumble like a dry cookie.

She'd already succumbed twice that week, her body staging a full-scale mutiny against her mind. All it took was him pulling her into an innocent hug after dinner, and the flame reignited, her defenses going up in smoke.

Everything about him was a walking, talking seduction, and her body always won the war.

When it started treading beyond the physical, she knew she was in trouble.

One afternoon, a sound she hadn't heard in years drifted from the living room. It was coming from the piano—her grandmother's old, dusty inheritance she'd never had the heart to get rid of, its keys being coaxed into a soft, soulful melody.

She crept out of her office, her heart thumping, to see Ezra at the bench, his long fingers moving over the ivory with a fluid, innate familiarity that made no sense.

And then he sang.

She'd heard him sing before. But this was different. His voice was a smooth, perfect tenor, wrapping around the lyrics of Babyface's "And Our Feelings" with a longing that was almost tangible.

He wasn't just playing a song; he was telling their story, a story she had never written, with a skill she had never imagined for him.

And when he hit that high note—*ohhhhhh oh ohhhhhhhh oh ohhhhhhhhhh*—a jolt of something more than just lust shot through her. It was a feeling of a deep, aching recognition, like hearing a song her own soul had forgotten.

The music stopped. He looked over his shoulder, having sensed her there.

"I didn't know you could play. Or sing like that," she uttered, her voice strained.

"Neither did I," he answered honestly, a look of genuine wonder on his face. "It just ... it felt like it was already there."

He hit a few keys, slow, one at a time. "You said in one of your journals that music was your first love. Maybe that's why it comes so naturally to me."

And that's when the real terror hit her. This wasn't just a major crack in her "I created him" theory. This was proof of something deeper, something she couldn't control.

He was evolving, becoming more than the sum of her words. He was becoming a vessel for the parts of her own soul—the joy, the music, the effortless creation—that she had locked away after Terrance.

He wasn't just a man in her house. He was a reflection of her own heart, singing a song she'd fallen in love with long ago.

She was overwhelmed by it all.

An hour later, she was sitting on Zaria's couch.

"This man," she declared, her voice tight with panic. "This—I don't even know what to call him. He's more than I wrote. The things he can do, the way he's making me feel ... I've literally created my own beautiful monster, and I've lost all control."

"So, have you tried an exorcism?" Zaria deadpanned, taking a sip of her smoothie. The smirk was so frustratingly funny Raina couldn't help but laugh, a broken, helpless sound.

"Heifer, I'm serious! I really need help!"

"Look, outside of calling a priest, there ain't much I can do, girlfriend." Her tone softened. "Unless..."

"Unless what?" Raina leaned forward, desperation in her eyes.

She put on her "investigative" voice. "Okay, let's break down the facts. Fact one: you don't fear him physically—you're actually comfortable and hella attracted to him. Fact two: you're terrified he's going to break your heart. Conclusion: the problem isn't him, it's you. Your heart needs a distraction."

Raina's eyes rolled. "Zaria..."

"Listen! You know the saying. The best way to get over one man is to get under a new one—"

"That is *your* damn saying, not an actual proverb!"

Zaria laughed. "Okay, fine. You don't have to sleep with anyone. You just need to create a buffer. You need to date-date. Go out with Marcus again; he's asked about you twice. Get out from under Ezra's spell. As much as I like your magic boyfriend, I know as long as you're trapped in that place with him 24/7, you're going to slip. Hell, baby girl, you're already in free fall."

Raina started to protest, but Zaria held up a hand. "And I can't even lie. If I had a man at my place who cooked like a chef, cleaned like a drill sergeant, and gave me out of this world orgasms, I wouldn't be trying to get rid of him. I'd be trying to figure out how to bottle and sell that magic. But you're not me." She looked at Raina, her expression serious now. "You're scared, sis. I know you."

"Terrance took me out, Z," Raina whispered, the old pain still a festering wound. "I can't spiral like that again."

"I know," her friend soothed. "Which is why you need to take back your power."

That was it. That was the phrase that landed.

Power equaled control.

Buoyed by the idea she desperately needed to reclaim, she nodded. She would go with Zaria's plan. She would create a boundary so clear, so real, that not even a magical man could cross it.

When she made it home, the heaviness of the grocery bags she brought in was nothing compared to the weight of her decision.

Ezra started putting the groceries away with a domestic ease as he hummed the Dru Hill song that had become his favorite— the one he always seemed to hum in her presence, like muscle memory.

She watched him, and a war raged in her chest—the comfort of his presence battling the loud, screaming panic of her own fear.

She swallowed, fortifying her resolve.

"Hey, E. So… I'm thinking about taking Zaria's advice again," she said, trying to sound casual. "I'm thinking about going on another date with Marcus. I didn't really give him a fair chance last time."

The contentment on his face was wiped clean, replaced by a flash of hurt so potent it was like a physical blow. He held a box of pasta in his hands, his grip so tight the bones seemed to press against his skin.

"Why?" he demanded, his voice tight. "I know things have been tense with us, but after the nights we've spent together … I don't understand. I thought that all meant something."

"Meant what, Ezra?" she scoffed, the sound harsh in the quiet room. "That we have an insane physical connection? We do. But that's not what a relationship is built on. At most, this is nothing more than us just passing the time until—"

"It's more than physical and you know it," he interjected, his voice dangerously low. He shoved the pasta box in the cabinet, and his calm fractured as he shut the door with a sharp, definitive click.

"It's about the way you look at me when you think I'm not paying attention. It's about the way your spirit responds to mine before your brain can build a wall. You can't tell me you don't feel it, too."

The cornered, terrified part of her brain took over, the part that knew how to burn bridges to keep from getting hurt.

"My feelings aren't the issue!" she shouted, the words tasting like ash. "The issue is that none of this is real. Because you're not real!"

The words slipped out before she could stop them—and as soon as they did, she wanted to claw them back.

She saw him flinch as if she'd physically slashed him, and a part of her own heart broke with the sight. She hadn't meant to cut him so deeply. And she didn't know how to stop the bleeding.

Before he could respond, she barreled on, the words tumbling out in a frantic, desperate attempt to justify the wound she'd just inflicted.

"Ezra, listen to me. What we have in here," she gestured around the apartment, her voice pleading, "it's amazing. It's like nothing I've ever experienced. But I have to be logical. This isn't a life; it's a beautiful, perfect bubble. I can't go on dates with you, I can't introduce you to my family, I can't walk down the street holding your hand. My whole world is shrinking to these four walls."

She took a shaky breath; the next part was even harder to say. "And what happens when the bubble pops? If this magic wears off and you're just ... gone? If I let myself fall completely for a man I can't even build a real life with, and then you disappear? That will destroy me. Don't you see? I can't survive that kind of heartbreak again."

The silence that followed was absolute, broken only by his slow, sharp intake of breath. He stared at her, his kind eyes shattered. For a moment, she thought he might dissolve right then, that the sheer force of her logic would unmake him.

Instead, he closed the distance between them in two short strides. But he didn't touch her.

She felt the heat radiating from his body, inhaled the freshness of his skin.

Then, his hand came up, cupping her chin, his thumb stroking her cheek in a gesture of agonizing tenderness.

"You keep saying I'm not real—" he spoke low, his voice thick with an emotion so authentic it tore her apart. He leaned in and kissed her—a searing, deep kiss that wasn't about passion, but about proof. It was a kiss of salt and sorrow that said, *Feel this. Feel me. How can this not be real?*

He broke off as abruptly as he had begun, leaving her lips tingling and her body trembling. His eyes said everything his mouth didn't as they held hers.

It was a look of love, of pain, and of a heartbreaking understanding of her fear.

Then he turned and strode into the guest room, closing the door firmly behind him.

The subtle click of the latch was the only sound.

Raina stood alone in the kitchen, shaken to her very core, the ghost of his kiss a burning testament on her lips.

chapter
twelve

TWO DAYS. Forty-eight hours of a silence so heavy it felt like a physical weight, pressing down on Raina's chest until it was hard to breathe.

They moved around the apartment like ghosts, two satellites knocked from their shared orbit, close enough to sense the pull but never touching.

The distance was a higher price than she could bear to pay.

On the third day, she saw him through the small opening of the door to his room. He was sitting on the edge of his bed, staring at his hands as if they were foreign objects. The mournful, pleading notes of Sisqo's "Incomplete" drifted from his Bluetooth, a soundtrack to his own quiet, existential crisis.

The music, that vacant stare, the very posture of him ... it was a man hollowed out by a grief he didn't have words for, and the sight of it broke through her resolve.

She nudged the door open fully and leaned against the frame. He looked up, his eyes wary, the warm light in them still shuttered from their fight.

"Ezra," she started, her voice shaky. "I ... I'm sorry."

He just watched her, his silence a patient, waiting wall.

"What I said ... it was brutal," she continued, stepping into the room. "It was a defense mechanism. It's what I do when I'm scared. I burn things down before they have a chance to burn me."

She sat on the bed, a careful foot of space between them. "Please see this from my point of view. I wasn't trying to hurt you. But to me, you're ... you're someone I made up on a Tuesday night after a bottle of wine. I was writing a book, and creating a character who I thought was the perfect man—for another character."

She shook her head, the incredible weight of her actions still sitting heavy on her concept of reality.

"I don't know what any of this means," she continued, her voice subdued. "I don't know the rules of this impossible thing that I've done."

He spoke after a brief pause, his voice rough with disuse. "You want rules, Raina? The only rule that should matter is that I'm here—now. Regardless of how."

He met her gaze, his own eyes burning with a new fire.

"You say I'm not real. But I can hold you. I taste the food you cook. I feel like shit each time you walk away from me." He turned to face her fully, the intensity in his gaze making her heart lurch. "And I love you. Tell me how any of that's not real."

The words, so direct and certain, stole her breath. But even that was part of the fantasy. He knew the words because she gave them to him.

That realization pushed her to fall back on her old, safe logic, the one that had protected her for six long years.

"You only think you love me because I wrote you that way," she countered. "It's part of your ... programming."

A sad, knowing smile touched his lips, but it never reached his eyes. "Check your draft, baby," he said, his voice soft but resonant with his own unshakeable truth. "There's nothing about love in there. You described a body. A few personality traits. You *wrote* the man." He leaned in, his proximity a warm, undeniable presence that made her skin tingle. "I *chose* to love the woman."

The words exploded in the quiet room, obliterating her carefully constructed arguments.

He *chose* love. It wasn't a line of code; it was a decision.

Her mind reeled, unable to process his claim of choice. It was too big, too terrifying. So, she doubled down on the logic of her own creative process.

Ezra wasn't choosing to love her; he was simply following the blueprint. She had written him to desire his protagonist with an overwhelming carnal pull. Therefore, what he felt for her—his author—could only be a misdirected echo of that programmed lust.

If she could prove it, if she could reduce this soul-deep connection to a simple, physical glitch, then it was something she could manage. Something she could control.

She surged across the space between them, crushing her mouth to his in raw defiance, determined to silence his heartbreaking logic with the fierce demand of her lips.

It wasn't a kiss of affection; it was meant to be *her* proof. A desperate, demanding collision meant to demonstrate his "choice" was nothing more than a program she could override.

He's just a body, her mind chanted, a frantic mantra against the deepening kiss. *Just a program reacting to me.*

His hands gripped her waist, pulling her onto his lap.

That's it, she thought to herself.

This had to be a battle, a war she could win by reducing him to a series of predictable, physical responses.

She ground against him, a frenetic maneuver to make him lose control, to become the simple, lust-driven creature she'd designed. If he would just get angry, get rough, get lost in the sex ... then she could prove even to him what this was.

But suddenly, Ezra's hands softened at her waist—no longer gripping—but holding her with excruciating tenderness, a move that instantly dismantled her frantic aggression with its warmth.

He wasn't breaking. He wasn't becoming the inferno she was trying to start.

And when his lips gentled against hers, turning their fever-pitched kiss into a slow, meaningful exchange, she knew with certainty that her experiment was failing.

He was no longer reacting to her body; he was responding to her pain. And that softness, that unwritten, chosen gentleness, was her undoing.

This wasn't physical—not even close. It was a spiritual resonance, connecting to places that had been locked away for years. Every gentle stroke of his thumb against her cheek felt like it was healing a part of her she didn't know was broken.

He gingerly lifted her and laid her on the bed.

He undressed her with reverence, and when he finally entered her, it was with a slow, methodical adoration that made her weep from the depths of her wounded heart.

And when she came, it was nothing like she'd ever experienced. It was the same subtle flutter that began between her eyebrows, but this time with a spark that traveled through her entire being with a total unraveling.

It was a climax of the soul.

And as the rapture crested, it brought years of unshed grief with it, leaving her shattered, her body trembling with a release so intense it felt like an ascension.

"I got you, baby," he whispered into her ear, holding her tight as she shook with the hardest, most cleansing cry of her life.

When their bodies finally relaxed, after he'd kissed the salt from her cheeks, they were still intimately connected as he lay inside her. He brushed the damp hair from her temple, his voice thick with emotion.

"Do you still believe this is just a part of my programming?"

The truth was a sob caught in her throat. She pulled away just enough to look at him, her eyes blurry with tears.

"No," she admitted, the word a painful concession. "It's so much more." Her voice cracked. "But that makes it worse, Ezra. Don't you see it?"

The reality of their situation came crashing back in as she sat up, pulling the sheet around her like a shield.

"Even if I let myself love you," she said, her voice strained as her eyes scanned the room, "what kind of life can we have? We can't leave this apartment. We could never take a vacation, we can't argue over who has to drive home, we can't just ... *be*. What kind of existence is that?"

The pain that flashed across his face was sharp and immediate, a mask of heartbreak before he smoothed it away, leaving nothing but a quiet, hollow emptiness. He had no answer for her.

She couldn't stand seeing the hurt in his eyes. She slid off the bed, pulling her clothes back on with jerky, clumsy movements, the vulnerability suddenly too much to bear.

She left the room without another word, without looking back, the weight of her impossible question—what kind of existence is that—sucking all the air from the space behind her.

Ezra

Ezra watched her go, the spot where she had been a warm, perfect fit now a cold ache beside him. Her question reverberated in his head.

What kind of existence is that?

She was right. She deserved so much more. She deserved the world. Not just the world within this apartment.

A new, fierce resolve hardened in his chest. His love for her wasn't a passive feeling, despite what she believed—it was one that demanded action.

He wasn't a robot she made. He wasn't some programmable AI come to life. He wasn't created to be a comfort; he was drawn here for a purpose. And that purpose was to do more than just love her from the couch.

He grabbed his phone off the nightstand, his thumb hovering over the two contacts listed there.

There was only one person who might be able to help him answer Raina's devastating question. He pressed 'call.'

"Ms. Oleta?" he said when she picked up. "It's Ezra. I need your help."

Half an hour later, after Raina had left to meet Zaria, he found Ms. Oleta on the balcony watering her plants.

He didn't waste time with pleasantries; the ache in his chest was too raw.

"She needs a life I can't give her from here," he said, his voice heavy. "A real life that includes going outside of these walls. Is there a way? A way to break the tether to this apartment?"

Ms. Oleta put her watering can down, her eyes filling with a deep sorrow as she looked out over the city. "I knew this day was coming."

She sighed, pulling a cigarette from her pocket and lighting it. "Every magic has a price, Ezra," she began softly. "The magic that binds you here is the same magic that sustains you." She looked at him, her gaze heavy. "As I see it, you have two paths before you. Neither of them is easy."

"Tell me," he urged, his voice full of desperate hope.

She paused for a moment, closed her eyes, then looked at him.

"The first path is the one you're on. It's the Path of the Anchor. You can stay in this world. You can be her comfort, her lover, her companion within these four walls ... possibly forever. As long as you stay connected to your source, you will remain solid."

Ezra nodded, his eyes dimming as he slowly inhaled, then exhaled audibly.

Ms. Oleta looked at him with a sad understanding. "But you know what that means. You will be her beautiful, perfect cage. She will love you, but your lives together will never grow beyond this balcony. She will never have the full, vibrant life she deserves out there."

Ezra flinched, the truth of her words a mirror to Raina's exact fear.

"Then there's the second path," she continued. "The Path of the Echo."

She looked out at the city lights, as if debating whether to share more. Then, she went on.

"There is another kind of magic connected to the Path of the Echo. A deeper, more costly kind. You can trade this physical form—the body you manifested into—for a different kind of permanence. You can sever the anchor to this place ... and re-tie the rope to her heart."

"What does that mean?" he murmured, his own heart pounding in his chest.

"It means you would become what you truly are," she said, her voice gentle. "A Heart's Echo. You would give up this body, but your soul, your love ... it would become a part of her. She would carry you with her always, wherever she goes. A feeling of warmth when she's lonely. A whisper of courage when she's scared."

Ms. Oleta turned to him, her eyes shining with unshed tears. "For a small window of time, you'd be able to leave this place, these four walls. You could be in the world with her, experience everything she does. But, when the time comes..."

Ezra's heart dropped. "I'd no longer exist."

"Yes—and no," she corrected.

Disbelief and pain filled his sharp, humorless laugh as his eyes widened. Looking away from her, he shook his head. "Stay and risk losing the woman I love because I can't give her what she needs? Or, vanish and—" The words caught in his throat, the wild laughter ceasing.

"You would be setting her free, child," Ms. Oleta interjected gently. "Giving her the courage and the strength she needs to live and love again, without fear. But..." Her voice was strained with resignation. "... after the final moment, you could never physically touch her again. You would exist only as an echo within her heart. You would be giving her everything she needs ... by giving up the one thing you want most."

Ezra looked down at his hands—hands that had held Raina less than an hour ago, that had comforted her, that had made her cry out his name.

He looked out at the vast city, the lights a glittering, distant tapestry. He thought of her trapped inside the very sanctuary he had become, and the realization broke his heart.

The choice was obvious. It was devastating. But it was his to make.

He had been created from her need for a love that wouldn't hurt her.

But he was choosing, with his own free will, to become the love that would heal her.

He finally looked at Ms. Oleta, his expression no longer hopeful or desperate, but full of a quiet, steel-edged certainty.

"How do we do it?"

chapter
thirteen

THE NEXT DAY, the silence in the apartment continued to be a heavy, suffocating presence between them. Raina tried to write, staring at the words on her screen until they blurred into meaningless shapes.

Her heart ached with a loneliness that was somehow sharper even though she wasn't alone. Ezra was there, a quiet, wounded ghost in the guest room, and the chasm between them was as wide as an ocean.

As evening approached and she was debating if she should have leftover pizza, Ezra appeared in the doorway of her office. He was dressed in the simple black button-down shirt and dark jeans she loved, his expression calm and unreadable.

"Get dressed, Raina Simone," he announced, his voice soft but firm. "I'm taking you out to dinner tonight."

She tried to laugh, but the sound that came out was humorless and thin. The tragic irony was that he wasn't trying to be cruel —his words were just a sweet joke landing on an exposed nerve.

"And where are you taking me, Ezra? To the good chair in the dining room? A romantic tour of the balcony?"

He smiled, a small, mysterious grin. He held out his hand, and she took it, standing to walk into his open arms. He wrapped them around her, then kissed the tip of her nose.

"No. I'm taking you somewhere real. Outside of here, with other people, and I won't be talking about pet dogs." He paused, his eyes full of a strange, powerful light. "Just trust me. And wear the navy blue dress."

He was gone before she could form a reply. A part of her wanted to dismiss it, to stay put in her misery. *This is a game,* she thought. *A well-meaning romantic fantasy he's built to make me feel better.*

He couldn't leave the house. She knew he couldn't. The barrier was real.

But the certainty in his voice, the look in his eyes ... it felt like a promise.

"Well," she said as she shut down her computer. "At least he keeps it interesting."

A few minutes later, she stood before her open closet, the scent of cedar and laundry detergent a small, normal comfort in a world that had gone sideways.

This is insane, a voice in her head screamed. *You're getting dressed up for a delusion. You're going to put on this dress, and he's going to lead you to the dining table, and you'll have to pretend your heart isn't breaking all over again.*

But another, quieter part of her—the part that had felt his arms around her, that had heard the hope in his voice— couldn't refuse his request.

Fine. She would play along with his beautiful, impossible delusion.

For one night.

He had asked for the navy blue dress. The request was basic, a sweet callback to a night he remembered with fondness. She pulled it off the hanger, the ribbed fabric feeling heavier in her hands than it looked.

To him, it was just a pretty dress. To her, it was armor, meant to project an aura of detachment. It was always worn on first dates, meant to be a silent statement: *I am good where I'm at. I don't need this to go well.*

The irony—the secret joke that only she was in on—was that Ezra was admiring her best defense against the shallow, performative world of dating. A shield, admittedly, that was useless against him, the man who had been created from the very vulnerability she was trying so desperately to hide.

At her vanity, she applied her makeup like a warrior putting on war paint. A sweep of bronze eyeshadow, a sharp line of eyeliner to define her dark, almond-shaped eyes, and a coat of rosy-brown gloss that gave her full lips a soft, kissable sheen.

She stared at her reflection. She looked ready for anything. She just wasn't sure what 'anything' was.

Taking a steadying breath, she stepped out of her bedroom.

Ezra was standing by the front door, waiting. The sight of him stole the air from her lungs.

He had changed clothes. The casual black button-down was gone, replaced by a crisp, white one. He wore black slacks that made him look impossibly elegant, the black wingtip shoes gleaming.

She smiled—these were all the items she'd impulsively added to her cart during their late-night online shopping spree when he had teased: "you didn't write me no clothes, Raina Simone."

When he finally looked up and his eyes met hers, she saw his own breath catch.

She approached slowly, waiting for him to lead her to the living room. When she realized he wasn't moving from the door, she gestured at it. "You're seriously going to try this again?"

He winked, an assured smile plastered on his face. "I told you," he said, his eyes never leaving hers. "Just trust me."

He turned and reached for the doorknob. It was a slow, deliberate movement that seemed to stretch time until it was thin and taut. Raina held her breath.

What is he doing?

He twisted it, the familiar click sounding like a cannon in the silent apartment. He swung the door open.

Then he stepped through the threshold ... and into the hallway.

Ezra

There she is.

The thought was a burst of relief when she came out of her bedroom. He had watched her retreat into the room earlier, and a part of him—a small, insecure part still healing from the wounds of her emotional whiplash—had feared she wouldn't come back out.

But she did. And she was wearing the dress.

He knew she saw it as her shield, a familiar uniform for the strange battlefield of dating.

He saw something else entirely.

He saw the way the ribbed fabric traced the gentle curve of her hips, the swell of her breasts, the soft line of her shoulders. It didn't look like armor to him. It looked like an elegant promise.

He saw past the makeup, seeing the way her eyes held all the stories she'd ever written and all the ones she was still afraid to live.

He saw the soft sheen on her full lips and remembered, with a jolt that was both sweet and agonizing, what it felt like to kiss her.

He didn't see a woman preparing for a fantasy tonight. He saw a woman taking a terrifying, beautiful chance.

After a lifetime of bad dates and broken hearts that had left scars on her soul—scars he could feel even if he couldn't see them—she was standing here, vulnerable and brave, ready to take a chance on him. On them.

And he would not hesitate to show her it was worth it.

After her sarcastic question—"you're seriously going to try this again?"—his heart thudded in his chest as he reached for the doorknob.

He stepped through the threshold and into the hallway.

The air was different out here. It was stale—the scent of old carpet mixed with the smells of Ms. Oleta's cooking—faint notes of garlic and onion. It was nothing like the clean, vanilla-scented air of Raina's unit.

It was ugly. It was mundane. And it was glorious. Every nerve in the soles of his feet seemed to awaken to the rough texture of the stiff hallway carpet.

I am definitely real. And I am here—outside the apartment.

He turned back to Raina. She was frozen on the other side of the threshold, her face a mask of pure, shattered disbelief. He watched her rush forward, her hand flying out to touch the space where his shimmering golden wall used to be. She looked from the empty doorway to him, her mouth opening and closing with no sound.

"How?" The word finally escaped her, a strangled, fragile whisper.

He couldn't stop the smile that spread across his face, a triumphant grin—for her. He reached back through the doorway and took her hand.

"I told the universe I needed help," he said, his thumb stroking her knuckles. "Ms. Oleta ... she helped me answer your question." He squeezed her hand gently. "The details can wait. Tonight is for us. Tonight is our first proper date."

A sensory explosion—that was the only way to describe it.

First, he was met with the openness of the Chicago night air, and he breathed in the mugginess of August.

Every sensation that followed was an up-close and personal first: the sight of a train rumbling overhead, the blur of headlights painting streaks on the pavement, a dozen different smells he couldn't name.

The lights were a galaxy of neon lettering and figures on glass, street-lamps that stretched into the sky, and for a moment, he was lost in the sheer, remarkable muchness of it all.

Then Raina's hand found his, a warm, solid anchor in the beautiful madness, and the world clicked into focus around her. The simple, public act sent a jolt of pure, possessive joy through him.

He looked at her, and her smile filled him with so much joy and love he thought he'd burst right there.

She is with me. Out here. In the world.

The Italian restaurant Ms. Oleta recommended was a haven of warmth and flickering light. He watched, mesmerized, as another couple laughed, their wine glasses clinking together—a small, perfect moment of human connection he had only seen on video, but was now a part of.

The first bite of authentic Italian pasta was a revelation. It wasn't a single flavor, but a cascade of them hitting his senses at once: the sharp, electric tang of sun-ripened tomato, followed by the deep, satisfying chew of the al dente noodle. It was complex, and simple, and perfect. A low groan of pleasure rumbled deep in his chest.

This is what it means to be fully alive.

But nothing compared to the sight of Raina sitting across from him. Her face was animated, her guard down completely as she told him stories about her childhood and her crazy, failed dates.

He watched her laugh, a real, from-the-belly laugh, at his observations. Each sound, each smile from her, was like fuel for his soul. He could feel it filling him up, even as he simultaneously felt his energy draining away at an imperceptible rate.

But he ignored it. This moment, and every moment he was allowed to have with her, was worth the deficit.

And he drank her in, memorizing the way the candlelight danced in her dark brown eyes, the way her lips curved when she smiled.

The entire world was a dizzying marvel, but she was its center. She was the only thing that mattered.

Late that night, as the date ended and they got out of the car, a wave of exhaustion hit him so suddenly his legs buckled. He caught himself on the vehicle door, forcing a quick laugh. "Whoa," he chuckled. "The real world is tiring."

Raina laughed with him. But in his mind, an icy voice whispered the truth.

The first payment is due.

An unnatural chill seeped into his skin as he took her hand to help her onto the curb, a cold so different from the vibrant warmth of hers. Ms. Oleta's words were an echo in his head: "... you'll be burning the candle away to buy yourself a few perfect days."

He watched the candlelight from the date fade from Raina's eyes, replaced by a flicker of confusion as she felt the cold radiating from his hand. She masked it quickly, choosing to believe in the night's magic.

He had bought her this. This laughter, this memory, this answer to her impossible question. He had paid for it with a piece of himself.

And as they walked back into the building, hand in hand, he felt the hollowness where the warmth used to be and knew, with a certainty as strong as his love for her, that he would go bankrupt for a thousand more nights just like it.

chapter
fourteen

THE MORNING after their magical first date wasn't a hangover, but a healing. Raina woke slowly, tangled in sheets that smelled not just of her, but of him—that impossible mix of shea butter body wash and a scent that was uniquely him.

The dinner, the dancing at a local club, the lovemaking after ... it was like a wonderful fantasy. But the solid, warm man sleeping beside her was undeniably real.

Ezra normally awakened before her, but today, he slept soundly, his face peaceful in the soft morning light. She watched the slow, even rhythm of his breathing—the rise and fall of his chest, the soft puff of air from his lips.

Breathe in. Breathe out.

He was breathing. That simple biological fact hit differently this morning. He wasn't just a presence in her apartment; he was a living, breathing man in her bed.

And if he was real enough to breathe, to hold her, to make her feel *all of this* ... then maybe everything else could be real, too.

And now, through some miracle pulled off by Ms. Oleta, he could join her in the world. She chuckled softly at the memory of him dancing at the club last night, the crowd eating up the Chris Brown moves he learned on TikTok.

A single, joyous tear fell and landed on his cheek. His eyes fluttered open, finding hers instantly.

"I'm sorry, baby," she whispered, her voice thick with emotion as she gently kissed the tear away. "Go back to sleep. You must be exhausted."

He stirred, a low hum in his chest, and shifted to wrap her in his arms, pulling her flush against him. He squeezed her, moaning into her neck like a man who had finally come home.

"No," he murmured. "I'm good. Waking up to you is all the energy I need." He kissed her then, a slow, deep, morning kiss full of unspoken promises.

"Okay, I have to know," Raina said when they broke apart, her eyes shining with excitement. "How did she do it? The door ... the entire night ... how?"

He laughed, a throaty, joyful sound. "Let's get some coffee in you. And I'll tell you everything."

He leaped from the bed with boundless energy, which sent a fresh thrill through her.

As she followed him to the kitchen, she realized for the first time in years, she didn't need coffee to get her day started. She was already buzzing with unfettered hope.

~

Ezra

As they sat at the breakfast nook, mugs cradled in their hands, Raina's smile was so bright it seemed to light up the whole room. And watching her, Ezra's heart exploded with a love so deep it was almost painful. He saw the hopeful, fragile light in her eyes, the way she looked at him as if he were the answer to a prayer.

And he knew, with a soul-crushing certainty, that he could not tell her the whole truth.

He couldn't tell her that every moment of their wonderful freedom was a grain of sand slipping through the hourglass of his existence. He couldn't bear to watch that light in her eyes extinguish.

So he gave her a piece of the truth, wrapped in a beautiful, necessary lie.

"Ms. Oleta unlocked the key," he said, his voice laced with a confidence that was pure performance. "She said the love between us—the one I chose and ... the one you're finally ready to embrace," he smiled, gently touching the tip of her nose, "created its own kind of magic. A new anchor. She thinks ... she thinks it could be permanent."

Raina's exuberant laugh was contagious. She jumped up from her chair and wrapped her arms around his neck, kissing him soundly.

"Prove it," she challenged with a twinkle in her eye. "Let's make sure you didn't turn into a vampire or something and can only go out at night."

He laughed, a full, hearty sound, even as the lie sat like a stone in his gut. "Get dressed. We 'bout to be outside-outside."

And as she danced out of the room to get ready, his smile slowly faded. He hated himself for the charade. He hated that he was protecting her with a falsehood that had an expiration date.

But he would do it a thousand times over to keep that look of pure joy on her face for however many more sunrises this beautiful fiction would buy them.

❧

Raina got dressed with a giddy energy so unfamiliar it felt like it belonged to a teenager. Her movements were quick but deliberate, a woman rediscovering the half-forgotten ritual of getting ready for a date she actually wanted to be on.

The summer dress she picked was the color of a perfect afternoon sky, a vibrant blue sprinkled with a delicate pattern of tiny white and blush-pink blossoms.

The sleeveless, V-neck cut dipped low, showcasing the warm, smooth skin of her collarbone, while the fabric gathered at her waist before flaring out. A flirty slit ran up one thigh, the ruffled hem bouncing with a life of its own as she moved.

She pinned her curls up in a messy but elegant bun, letting a few tendrils frame her face. At her vanity, she moved with a rediscovered sense of purpose. It wasn't about hiding; it was about highlighting.

A sweep of bronze shadow made her warm, caramel skin glow, and a sharp, delicate line of black liner accentuated the shape of her eyes, bringing out the deep brown.

Her full lips, already a perfect canvas, were traced with a soft brown pencil and filled in with a nude gloss that shimmered just so.

She stared at her reflection, at the happy woman looking back. It was a face she hadn't seen in years—hopeful, a little hesitant, but ready for the world.

When she stepped into the living room, Ezra was sitting on the couch, his head leaning back against the cushion, his eyes closed as if savoring a quiet moment.

"You okay, babe?" she asked, a flicker of her concern from last night returning.

His eyes snapped open, and the moment they landed on her, a slow, appreciative grin spread across his face as he drank her in.

"Damn," he crooned, his gaze gliding over her from head to toe. "I am more than okay, Raina Simone."

They strolled to The Grind, Raina and Zaria's usual coffee spot. The simple act of walking down a public street holding his hand was so overwhelmingly normal it was no longer like a fantasy.

The sun beamed its approval on them, and for the first time, Raina accepted that not only was this real—but it was possible.

Ezra was in a continued state of sensory overload. The sudden, angry blast of a car horn, followed by a man shouting cuss words out of his window to another driver, made him jump. Raina just laughed.

"Is that ... normal?" He looked back at the chaos with a half-smirk, his eyes wide and curious.

"Painfully normal," she confirmed, squeezing his hand.

The rich smell of dark roasted coffee greeted them a half-block before they even reached the cafe. When the hostess smiled at him and asked if they preferred to dine inside or out, Ezra was so mesmerized by the simple, human interaction that Raina had to answer for them.

They chose a small table outside.

He read the menu with the focused intensity of a scholar deciphering an ancient text. He didn't know what half the things were, but he was excited to try everything.

When the waitress came to take their order, Raina had just stepped away to the ladies' room. When she returned, she saw the woman jotting down the last of Ezra's requests.

"Okay," the waitress said with a smile, turning her attention to Raina as she sat down. "So just to confirm for you, ma'am, we have the large latte with vanilla and caramel, and the breakfast scramble with American cheese, peppers, and extra bacon?"

Raina's eyes snapped to Ezra. He just gave her a small, knowing smile, a silent "I got you." She looked back at the waitress, a slow, genuine grin spreading across her own face. "That," she said, her voice full of warmth, "is absolutely perfect."

The breakfast date was basic. It was by all accounts boring. And it was the most magical hour of her life. They talked about nothing and everything, his eyes full of wonder as he experienced the world, up close, for the first time in daylight.

Her heart was so filled with a fierce love she could barely breathe.

The next day, Raina heard Ezra singing in the shower, her heart doing a slow, complicated dance in her chest. The joy of the previous day and the night before that was a warm, living thing, but his exhaustion was a cold flow of worry she couldn't ignore.

Both times they'd gone out, he was near collapsing when they got back home. Although he recovered quickly after sitting for a while, it was still concerning.

He can't just burn himself out for me, she thought. He needed a day of rest. A day of just … being.

An idea sparked, one that was both exciting and terrifying. She tiptoed into the bathroom, where the steam was already fogging the mirror.

"Babe," she said, her voice bubbling with elation. "I have a great idea. Let's have a lazy day today. We can order food, binge movies… and we should invite Zaria. She has to meet you for real!"

The shower curtain slid back. Ezra's skin glistened with water droplets, a wide grin on his face. "I think that's a perfect idea, baby." His smile turned devilish, his eyes roaming over her. "You know what else I think is perfect?"

"What's that?" she asked with a knowing smirk.

"You." He held out a wet hand to her. "Get your fine, perfect ass in this shower with me, woman."

He didn't have to ask twice.

She grinned, and after quickly disrobing, placed her hand in his—but blinked. Once again, his skin was cooler than usual. Not cold exactly, but the contrast made her pause.

"Your hands are chilly," she acknowledged, trying to keep her voice light as she stepped in with him.

He smiled, pulling her in closer. "Then come warm me up."

She shook off the worry. It was probably just the AC or the cool tile beneath his feet.

Nothing more.

But a tiny voice in the back of her mind whispered, *Keep an eye on him.*

Later that afternoon, when Raina opened the door for Zaria, the anticipation was thick.

She crept in, her eyes already wide and doing a full investigative sweep of the room. Her gaze landed on Ezra, who was standing in the middle of the living room, a picture of casual confidence in a graphic tee and cargo shorts.

Raina watched her best friend process the impossible. She saw the flicker of awe, the dawning recognition, and a healthy dose of pure shock as Zaria took him in, from his crown of coils down to his bare feet.

Ezra, for his part, just smiled, his arms opening in a friendly, "bring it in" gesture.

She walked over slowly, her eyes still the size of saucers. She allowed him to envelop her in a warm hug, and when he lifted her a few inches off the floor with a playful squeeze, a choked laugh escaped her.

"Oh my God," she said, breathless, her eyes meeting Raina's over his shoulder. "You really are... real. And huge!"

Raina yelped and clapped, a moment of pure joy overcoming her.

As they prepared popcorn and snacks for the movie marathon, Zaria grilled Ezra with the precision of a seasoned investigator looking out for her best friend.

He took it all in stride, answering her questions with a charm and wit that had her hooked within the hour. More than once, she shot Raina a look from across the kitchen island that said, "Okay, girl, this is the one."

Finally, they all piled onto the couch and binged classic Denzel flicks. In a quiet moment while they were switching movies and Ezra was in the kitchen getting more drinks, Zaria leaned in close to Raina.

"Okay, I'm sold. He's perfect," she whispered. "Which means you have to bring him to my wedding next spring." She paused, her expression turning serious. "So ... what's the story we're telling yours and my family about how you two met? Did you meet at the bookstore? At a bar? Because 'my bestie manifested him with wine and a Word doc' probably will not fly with my Auntie Gertrude. She'll be bathing you both in holy water."

Raina laughed with Zaria, but just as quickly it faltered. The simple, practical question pierced the perfect, cozy bubble of the afternoon. It was a stark reminder that even with this miracle, their story had no logical place in the real world.

She glanced toward the kitchen, where she could hear Ezra happily humming his favorite song. "We ... we haven't thought that far ahead," she admitted. Then, a spark of her old, defiant spirit returned. "But hell, I'm a writer. I wrote *him*, didn't I? I can write us a fantastic origin story."

She winked at Zaria just as Ezra came back and sat between them on the couch, handing each of them a fresh drink.

He rubbed his hands together. "Alright ladies, what's next? Brown Sugar, Love and Basketball, Love Jones..."

The ladies looked at each other behind his back. Zaria just shook her head slowly, mouthing with wide, impressed eyes, "Oh, he's a keepa'!"

chapter
fifteen

EZRA

Ezra stepped out onto the balcony, the August air a welcome balm against his thrumming nerves. The last few days had been a dizzying, sun-drenched dream, a whirlwind of firsts that were both exhilarating and stunning.

He leaned against the railing, watching the city breathe below him, a world of light and sound that was now, impossibly, open to him.

For Raina.

Because of Raina.

His love for her wasn't just an emotion; it was his very purpose. And that purpose now had a price tag.

As he waited for her to get dressed, his mind drifted back to the conversation that had made this all possible, the quiet, heavy words exchanged on this very balcony with Ms. Oleta....

"How do we do it?" he'd asked with a desperate eagerness when she told him his desire to give Raina what she wanted was possible.

"I can lend you a piece of my own spirit to act as a temporary tether, to let you walk in the world with her. I can open the door for you."

"Then do it," he urged. "Please."

"But you have to understand," the old woman continued, her voice a gentle, heartbreaking warning. "The world outside runs on a different currency. It will demand payment for every moment of freedom. The magic I can give you is a borrowed light, baby. You're choosing to burn a stranger's candle at both ends. The flame will be twice as bright, but it will only last half as long.

Every laugh you share with her out there, every meal you taste, every time you hold her hand under the open sky ... it will take a piece of what makes you you. It will be irreversible. Are you sure that's a price you're willing to pay for a few perfect days?"

Suddenly, Ezra's focus snapped to something Ms. Oleta said. "Wait, you said I'd be burning your candle at both ends ... what will happen to you? I can't hurt you—"

She chuckled, her raspy voice echoing in the wind. "Baby, I'll be fine. I'm of this world, so the energy comes back. But it's not a free ride." She took a slow breath. "I'll be tired, yes. And I'll feel it all with you ... the good and the bad. The bright flame is beautiful, but it still burns. It's a small price I'm willing to pay for you both."

She smiled wide, her hand reaching up to touch his cheek in a gesture of kindness. "Stop worrying, Ezra. You're on a mission now."

The memory faded, but the weight of the choice settled in his soul. He could stop it all right now. Stay and keep Raina caged. Or, he could step outside and continue to give her the world, even if it cost him everything.

A subtle shimmer passed over his arm, and he stopped breathing for a moment as his gaze snapped down to his hand resting on the railing. It was gone in a second—just a flicker, like a heat wave or an old film reel—but the image was seared into his mind.

"Nah...it's just the light. I'm trippin', that's all. There's no way it can be happening this fast."

He flexed his fingers, a tremor of pure terror running through him before he forced it down, burying it deep.

The soft slide of the patio door pulled him from his thoughts. He turned, and there she was.

His Raina Simone.

Every ounce of his pain, his fear, his fresh, firsthand knowledge of the cost—all evaporated at the sight of her in her new summer dress.

With all other concerns and feelings stripped away, one constant remained: a love so profound, so absolute, it was the only real thing in the universe.

He had already made his choice. Now, he would enjoy every second of the borrowed time it bought them.

The last few days had been a whirlwind of joy and amazement. The miracle held. Every morning, Raina would wake with her heart in her throat, half-expecting the shimmering barrier to have returned, but the front door always opened to the mundane, beautiful freedom of the hallway.

Believing a genuine miracle had happened—that Ezra was now permanently, tangibly real—she did the one thing she had been fighting since Terrance: she let herself fall completely.

She made it her mission to show him the world. He, in turn, made it his to show her what it felt like to be adored within it.

Their first big outing was a picnic at Jackson Park on the south side. For Ezra, it was another moment of sensory exploration. He kicked off his shoes the moment they reached the expansive lawn, his bare feet sinking into the grass with a low groan of pure bliss.

"It's soft," he told her, as if he were giving a report, curling his toes in the cool, damp blades. "It feels alive."

When a black ant crawled onto his leg as they ate lunch on a blanket, the tickle of its tiny feet was a marvel. He didn't brush it away. Instead, he held out a finger, watching with fascinated curiosity as the insect explored the unfamiliar terrain of his knuckle.

He lay on his back for an hour, captivated by the clouds drifting across the vast blue canvas of the sky, describing their shapes to Raina with the seriousness of a seasoned art critic.

He discovered the rough, comforting texture of tree bark against his palms; the sun-warmed sweetness of wild cherries they found growing near a creek; the chaotic joy of watching a stranger's dog chase a bright red frisbee.

Raina watched him, her heart so full it felt like it might burst. He wasn't just seeing the world; he was experiencing the very concept of it. Looking at it all through his fresh, unjaded eyes made everything feel new and sacred to her, too.

The next day they visited the Art Institute. Raina had always found it a quiet, contemplative space. Through Ezra's eyes, it was a riot. He was overwhelmed by the sheer volume of color and history in every brushstroke. He stood before a Basquiat for ten full minutes, utterly silent, his head tilted as if listening.

"What do you see?" she whispered, standing beside him and wrapping her arms around his waist.

"There's so much," he answered, his voice full of awe. "It's like ... the color has a sound ... a temperature." He looked at her, his eyes wide with wonder. "Is this what art is? It's like your writing. It doesn't just show you something. It makes you feel something."

"Tomorrow," she told him as they drove home, "I'm taking you to my childhood fun place."

His eyes lit up. "Where is that?"

"You'll see," she winked with a wide grin.

The next day, she took him to one of her favorite places to experience the sheer, glorious chaos of an amusement park. Even the hour-long drive was its own kind of adventure. He stuck his arm out the car window, allowing the wind to breeze through his fingers.

"I so love to see you enjoying yourself," Raina said, glancing over at him. "There's so much more I want to show you."

He smiled at her. "I love you, baby."

"Love you, too," she beamed, returning her focus to the road.

When they made it to Six Flags, the flashing lights, the cacophony of delighted screams and ringing bells, and the sticky-sweet smell of cotton candy clung to the air.

Ezra rode his first rollercoaster, and the initial look of stark terror on his face melted into a wide-mouthed grin of unadulterated exhilaration that made Raina laugh until she cried.

He won her a giant, ridiculously plush stuffed sloth at a ring toss game, his focus so intense and unwavering you'd think he was defusing a bomb.

They ate greasy, perfect French fries and funnel cake. They shared a strawberry ice cream cone that dripped down their hands in the summer heat, and he insisted on licking the sweetness from her fingers, right there in the middle of the crowded park.

It was on a Ferris wheel that the moment of pure domestic couple-dom happened. On the ground while they waited for it to rise, a group of women laughed, their colorful dresses bright against the deepening dusk.

Ezra watched them, then turned to Raina with a teasing, mischievous glint in his eyes. "You know," he said, his voice a low drawl. "Now that I'm out in the world, I see I have ... options. Maybe I could try dating one of them?"

Raina, who had been leaning blissfully against his shoulder, shot upright. A possessive fire she didn't know she had ignited in her chest.

"Don't you even think about it," she said, her voice a low warning, but a smile played on her lips. She poked him in the chest. "First of all, you are officially now and forever off the market. Trust me, boo, you don't want these problems. You are mine, and mine alone."

He threw his head back and laughed, a loud, joyous echo in the small carriage. He pulled her close, capturing her mouth in a deep kiss. "Good," he murmured against her lips. "Because you're the only problem I ever want to have."

In that moment, they weren't a woman and her manifested man. They were just Raina and Ezra. A real couple, teasing each other on a Ferris wheel, falling deeper in love with every shared laugh and stolen kiss.

After a few days of resting at home, which she insisted on because his growing exhaustion was becoming a bigger concern, she took him to a food festival in Grant Park. He was mesmerized, like a kid in a candy store, his head swiveling between the overwhelming selection of food tents and the vibrant pulse of a DJ playing classic House music.

It was there that a glimpse of a possible future ambushed Raina, putting her heart in a chokehold. A young couple nearby was struggling with a baby who was having a full-blown meltdown, its cries sharp and inconsolable. The parents looked exhausted, trying everything to soothe the screaming child.

Ezra observed them, his expression soft with an empathy that was purely him. He leaned over to the mother. "May I?" he asked, extending his hands.

The mother, frazzled and desperate, looked from Ezra's kind eyes to her screaming daughter. Before she could even answer, the little girl, who couldn't have been more than six months old, stopped crying mid-wail. Her tear-filled eyes locked on Ezra, and she reached for him with her tiny, chubby hands.

A stunned look passed between the parents. The mother hesitated for only a second before gently placing the beautiful brown baby into Ezra's waiting arms.

The second she was secure against his chest, she stared up at him, her little mouth forming a perfect 'o' of wonder.

He looked completely in his element, rocking the child with an innate gentleness, his voice a low, soothing hum.

Raina watched, her own breath caught in her throat. She'd never had a maternal urge in her life, had never pictured herself with children. But watching this powerful, gentle man so effortlessly calm a child, seeing the tender way he held her ... suddenly, her ovaries were singing a full-throated gospel hymn.

"Wow," the mother said, her voice full of exhausted awe. "That's ... a miracle. She usually hates strangers. Do you have children?"

Ezra was too busy cooing at the little girl, who now had a fist tangled in his shirt, a gummy smile on her face. "No, I don't have any children," he answered finally, without looking away from the baby. Then his eyes lifted and met Raina's over the child's head, and he gave her a soft, wistful smile that held a world of unspoken thoughts.

When he gently handed the baby back to her stunned parents, Raina linked her arm through his, holding on tight.

"That was ..." she started, but couldn't find the right word. "That baby was completely smitten with you."

He simply smiled, then turned, wrapping her in his arms, kissing her deeply. "I love you so much, Raina Simone," he declared, his eyes a clear mirror to his words.

The last of her walls crumbled to dust. "I love you, too," she responded, the admission coming out as natural as breathing.

She was living in the perfect lie, a beautiful, sun-soaked dream of a life she never thought she wanted.

And she refused to let herself believe, even for a second, that it would ever have to end.

chapter
sixteen

AFTER A PERFECT MONTAGE of perfect days, Raina woke up blissful, snuggled in his arms. The love was genuine, and a future seemed possible, like a warm, sun-filled road stretching out before them.

But as today—another day they had planned to stay home—wore on, she noticed small, dissonant notes in their perfect symphony.

It started with their lovemaking. It was as beautiful and tender as ever. But this morning, after the second time she'd cried out his name, he didn't just collapse against her.

His body went rigid for a moment, then trembled with a deep, unnerving shudder that had nothing to do with pleasure and everything to do with his growing exhaustion.

He was utterly spent. She held him, her fingers massaging his coils, her own bliss rapidly cooling as worry gripped her heart.

An hour later while making coffee, he stumbled. It was a small thing—a single misstep as he turned from the counter, mugs rattling in his hands. He caught himself, playing it off with a quick laugh.

"Guess I'm no longer a morning person," he winked, but she saw the smile was a mask, given away by the thin veil of fatigue in his eyes.

Throughout the day, the glitches became harder to ignore. He was quieter, his usual vibrant energy banked down to a soft, weary stillness.

She took his hand while they were watching a movie and felt it —a strange, low hum beneath his skin, like a barely there electrical current. It was the feeling of a machine running on low power.

She pulled her hand back, startled. "What was that?"

He looked at his own hand, confused. "What was what, baby?"

When she touched him again, it was gone.

The last crack in her denial came as he stood looking out the window. The setting sun backlit his form, and for a terrifying second, his silhouette seemed to thin, his entire body appearing to glow from within. It was a soft, golden radiance pulsing under his skin before quickly resolving back to the solid man she knew.

The beautiful, perfect lie was crumbling. The writer in her, the one who would peel back every layer to understand the world, needed to ask the question.

But the woman who loved this impossible man with a fury she'd never known was terrified of the answer.

Maybe this is just the natural part of his magic, she reasoned within herself. *He would tell me if something was wrong.*

That evening, she found him on the balcony. He wasn't just looking at the sunset; he seemed to be part of it. The deepening dusk made his form look almost translucent, as if a quiet, golden light was glowing just beneath his skin. And this time, it didn't fade.

These incidents were not tricks of the light. As beautiful as the imagery was, these were changes she could no longer ignore. She needed to know what was happening to him.

"Ezra." Her voice trembled, fear turning her blood to ice as she stepped into the cool night air. "Something's wrong. I can see it. Please, just talk to me."

He turned to her, and his face held a sorrow so vast it seemed to eclipse the city lights behind him. He could no longer protect her with the lie. "You were right, Raina," he said softly. "About our life together, about this joy. It's a bubble, baby. And it's about to pop."

"What do you mean?" she asked, though the cold dread coiling in her stomach already knew the answer.

"I lied to you," he admitted, his voice ragged with exhaustion. "After our last fight, I asked Ms. Oleta for help." His eyes brimming with tears, locked on her. "She warned me about the risks. She called it a trade."

Risks. A trade. The words snagged in Raina's mind.

"She said I would be trading my substance," he continued, his voice weakening, "my existence... for a walk in the world with you."

The cold skin. The exhaustion after sex. The stumbles. The hum. The moments of glowing.

Every small, strange detail from the last week clicked into place with horrifying clarity. These weren't just "glitches." It wasn't all in her head.

"Every moment outside," he rambled on like he was running out of time, and she saw him sway, gripping the railing for support. "Every day I walked with you under the sun… it was another grain of sand slipping through my fingers. Another piece of me … burning away to buy us more time."

"Ezra, baby," she said cautiously, fear overwhelming her. "You're scaring me. What have you done?"

He took a steadying breath as his form appeared to grow weaker. "I borrowed some of Ms. Oleta's magic … so I could spend time with you … before …"

"Before what?" Her mouth suddenly went dry as she asked the questions she was already forming the painful answers to.

"I couldn't let you live in a cage," he cried, being barely held up by the railing. "I couldn't stand the thought of you growing to resent me—"

Her mind went back to their last fight and the question she'd asked:

What kind of existence is that?

This was her fault. Her stupid, selfish fear had caused him to do something she couldn't comprehend. "No," she whispered, the denial a reflex. "No."

"I took the path of the Echo, baby."

Her own tears flowed. "What does that even mean?"

He looked out into the night sky. "It means I have to leave you, so I can become a part of you."

"What?! Why?!" she cried, surging forward and gripping his arms, as if her touch could physically anchor him to this world. "Why would you do something like this without telling me?!"

Her mind raced, a frantic search for a loophole.

"This stops now! Whatever was done, we stop it! You stay here with me. We stay here, inside, if that's what it takes. We can fix this! We can—"

He gave her a heartbreakingly gentle smile, reaching up to cup her cheek. His hand was so cold—an unnatural, absolute chill, a violation against her warm, tear-stained skin. "It's too late, baby," he said, and his form began to truly unravel.

She saw the golden light seep from the seams of his skin, strongest at his chest, like a star collapsing inward. Thin, bright cracks appeared along his arms, and she could hear a soft, whispering sound, like sand falling on glass. "The time— it's all been spent."

She looked on in horror, gingerly touching the cracks on his arm as if she could repair him.

Time, she thought with a terrified gasp. That was the currency. And he had already paid in full.

His knees buckled, and she caught him, his weight unusually light. She half-dragged him back inside and onto her bed. The light beneath his skin was brighter now, a soft, radiant pulse that made the floral pattern of her duvet visible right through the faint outline of his body.

"Ezra, please, just tell me how to fix this," she begged, her voice frantic. "Wait, I'll call Ms. Oleta—"

He used the last of his strength to grip her wrist, his touch firm. "She can't help us, baby," he rasped. "She told me the cost. I was willing to pay it."

"Ezra, baby! Why? Why did you do this to yourself?" She sobbed, her tears a hot, useless flood. "You shouldn't have sacrificed yourself for a few days outside."

"It wasn't just about having a few days outside," he whispered, his eyes locking on hers, pouring a lifetime of love into one last gaze. "It was for you. I love you more than this life, Raina Simone. I'm not sorry. I got to see you happy ... in your world. And it was beautiful."

His trembling was uncontrollable now. She could hear the hollowness in his voice, the way it seemed to echo from a great distance. She gasped through her own tears as sorrow wrecked her soul.

"I love you, Ezra," she choked, the words a painful, desperate confession. "I love you so much, baby. You can't leave me now. You can't!"

"I'm sorry if I ever caused you any discomfort," he breathed, the light from his chest pulsing harder now, in time with his weakening words. "I know it wasn't easy in the beginning."

She managed a small, watery smile as tears streamed down her face. "You're the only problem I ever want to have, remember?"

She leaned down and kissed him, and his lips were like ice.

"I'm ... so thirsty," he whispered, the words a papery, distant sound.

"Okay, baby, okay," she wept, pulling away. "I'll get you some water. Just hold on. Don't go anywhere. Please, hold on."

As she turned to flee, he called her name, his voice a mere thread of sound. "Raina ... get my journal..."

His cryptic words barely registered over the thundering in her ears. She sprinted to the kitchen, her movements frantic, her own sobs choking the air from her lungs.

Please, please, please, her mind chanted, a desperate prayer to a universe that had already cashed its check. She fumbled in the cabinet, her hands shaking so violently she could barely grip a glass.

The sound of the water blasting from the faucet was a roar, filling the suffocating silence.

As the glass overflowed, she heard it. Not with her ears, but somewhere deeper, in the center of her soul.

A faint, fading sound of his voice, imbued with his love, calling her name one last time.

"... Raina Simone ..."

"NOOOOO!" she screamed, leaving the water running, the glass dropping from her hand and shattering in the sink.

The single splintering sound was a gunshot signaling the end of a war she had already lost.

Water splashed from her trembling hands onto the floor as she sprinted back, her bare feet slipping on the hardwood.

She skidded to a halt in the doorway of her bedroom, her chest heaving, her eyes wild, ready to scream, to beg, to bargain.

The bed was empty.

A raw, feral denial clawed its way up her throat.

He must have fallen.

She scrambled to the other side of the bed.

But he wasn't there.

"Ezra?" she called out, her voice a shredded whisper.

The silence that answered was a physical blow.

She ran to the bathroom, flipping on the light to find it stark and empty.

She dashed back to the bedroom and dropped to her hands and knees and looked under the bed, her heart pounding a frantic, desperate prayer.

Please, please, please!

But there was nothing.

She clambered up and tore out of the room, searching the small condo like a madwoman, screaming his name now—a raw, ragged sound of pure panic.

"Ezra?!"

She ended up back in her bedroom doorway, her frenzied search yielding nothing but a deeper sense of emptiness.

The man she loved was gone.

The physical form—the broad shoulders, the warm skin, the hands that had held her—had just ... vanished.

But in the center of the room, hovering silently above her bed where he had just lain, was a shimmering, golden light. It looked like a small, captured sun, pulsing with a gentle, silent rhythm. It was the most beautiful, terrifying thing she had ever seen.

She stood frozen, a strangled sob caught in her throat. "What..."

The light seemed to respond to her voice. It pulsed once more, a soft, warm beat that resonated deep in her own chest. Then, it floated across the room—a slow, purposeful glide—and sank directly into her heart.

The impact didn't feel physical. There was no pain. There was only a sudden and overwhelming warmth that spread through her entire being, a wave of pure love so potent it buckled her knees.

And then, it was over. The golden light was gone.

The silence that rushed back in was absolute—like a physical, crushing weight.

And she was truly alone now.

Raina collapsed to her knees, throwing her arms over the bed where he had been, her world broken like the shards she left in the sink.

She let out a single, soul-shattering scream into the sudden, deafening void.

chapter
seventeen

WINE AND SLEEPING pills finally lulled Raina to sleep—
the only things that could dull her senses enough to make her
forget to cry.

The next morning, she woke up with her arm thrown across
the empty side of the bed, her body still seeking Ezra's
warmth.

The cold sheets were the first slap of reality. The second was
the crushing silence that rushed in to fill his place—roaring in
her ears.

There was no humming or singing coming from the kitchen.
No soft footsteps on the hardwood floor.

She didn't get out of bed right away. Instead, she rolled over,
burying her face in the pillow he slept on, inhaling for a trace
of his scent.

There was nothing. Just laundry detergent and the cold, sterile
smell of absence.

Panic clawed at her. She couldn't lose his presence, too.

She stumbled out of her bedroom and into the guest room—his room. She tore through his laundry hamper, grabbing a handful of his clothes and putting it to her face, inhaling him.

She grabbed the simple gray t-shirt he'd been wearing when he first appeared. She rubbed the soft cotton on her face and breathed him in again. It was all there—sandalwood, powder and something uniquely Ezra.

A wail tore from her chest, raw and ragged. She removed her own shirt and pulled his over her head, its worn fabric swallowing her whole.

She curled up on his bed, clutching the giant plush sloth he'd won for her, its cheerful, stitched-on smile a cruel mockery of the gaping hole in her heart.

She stayed like that for hours ... was it days? She couldn't grasp time anymore.

Zaria called, then texted, then finally let herself in with her spare key. She found Raina in his bed, a small shape lost in a too-big t-shirt, the only sound in the house the endless, looping chorus of Dru Hill's "Beauty."

"It was his favorite song," she cried out without preamble.

Zaria didn't speak. She just sat on the edge of the bed, a silent, steady anchor in Raina's storm, until her weeping softened into exhausted silence.

For a week, sleep wasn't a refuge; it was an abyss, a black, dreamless pit she fell into each night. She would wake up in his bed, groggy and hungover, the grief hitting her like a physical blow the moment the silence crept back in.

But last night was different.

She had dreamed.

There was no setting, only a warm, golden light, like the one that had sunk into her chest.

And Ezra.

He stood before her, looking exactly as she remembered—beautiful, real, his kind eyes full of a love that was a palpable, living thing.

He said nothing at first. He just held that gorgeous smile that had always melted her fears ... her resolve. He reached for her, his touch solid and warm, instantly calming the frantic beat of her heart. He brought her hand to his lips and kissed each fingertip, his gaze never leaving hers.

"My Raina Simone," he'd whispered. It was a greeting, a reassurance, an entire conversation packed into one perfect invocation.

She woke with a gasp, his name lingering on her lips. For a blissful, disoriented second, the dream was real. She could still feel the phantom warmth of his grip on her hand, could still hear the perfect echo of his voice in the room.

She reached for him.

But then the cold seeped in.

The space beside her was empty.

The apartment was silent.

Utterly, crushingly silent.

The contrast between the dream and the reality was a fresh, brutal wound.

But the dream ... it wasn't just a memory. It was a visit. A message.

Hope pierced through the fog of her grief.

He was created from her words, from the desperate magic of her own heart. The dream was proof that he was still in there, somewhere, an echo she could hear if she just listened hard enough.

If he can exist in my dreams, maybe ...

The thought was a lifeline.

... maybe he can exist on the page again.

She scrambled out of bed, her movements no longer sluggish with grief but sharp with a new, frantic purpose.

She ignored the pounding in her head and the stale taste of wine on her tongue. She tore open her laptop, the sudden bright light of the screen making her flinch.

She wrote frantically, page after page, trying to invoke the same passion she had felt that first night.

His description.

His voice.

His laugh.

But after an hour, all she had were words on a screen. The vessel was empty. The magic—born of a unique cocktail of pain and longing—was gone, replaced now by a love so vast it felt like its own form of grief.

Emotionally and physically drained, she gave up and wept.

Finally, when the weeping subsided into a fragile resolve, she found the strength to reach out to Ms. Oleta. She needed answers.

An hour later, the old woman sat next to Raina on the couch, her presence a heavy but comforting weight.

"Please, Ms. Oleta. I have to know what my Ezra was. And, what happened to him?"

Ms. Oleta's voice was gentle, full of sympathy. "What he was, baby, was a prayer. Your prayer. And what he is now ... is a part of you." She took Raina's hand. "He came to me, as you know. I told him about the two paths before him. The path where he could stay here, safe in this home, and love you forever. And the path where he could give that love back to you, as an ultimate gift, so you could be free."

Raina's eyes overflowed with a new gush of tears, her brows knitting in confusion.

Ms. Oleta gave a sad smile. "He chose to become what he was always meant to be. A true Heart's Echo. He didn't just disappear, Raina. He poured his entire being, every ounce of that impossible love, directly into your own heart.

The warmth in you? The courage you don't think you have yet? That's him. He didn't leave you. He just ... changed his address."

The old lady's smile widened, and it was the first time Raina had a desire to return one, small though it may be. Then, after a few seconds, with a weak voice, she said, "Please. Tell me how I can get him back."

A tear rolled down Ms. Oleta's cheek. "You can't, baby. That kind of magic don't offer round-trips. His love for you was so deep, he willingly made the trade."

"I didn't want him to go," Raina's voice was strained.

"I know, darlin'. He didn't want to leave—he had come to love this life. But when he realized you would be caged by his limitations, he sacrificed the desire to live so that he could give you those few moments of joy."

Her words were a comfort, but they were abstract. Raina's loss was still a sharp, physical void.

"He left something for you," Ms. Oleta said, her voice soft as she retrieved a familiar leather-bound journal from the bag she'd brought with her. "He gave this to me when he made the decision to follow his path, and asked me to give it to you when you were ready to hear from him one last time."

Raina's eyes widened as her trembling fingers wrapped around the recorded thoughts of her man, her mind tracing back to his final call before he disappeared.

... get my journal ...

Ms. Oleta stood to leave. She stopped at the door, looking back at Raina. "Ezra was a very special soul. And it takes another special soul to be able to call forth something like that from the universe."

Then, she left.

For another week, the journal sat on Raina's coffee table, unopened. It was a final goodbye she wasn't ready for.

But after another day of barely eating, and barely moving, she knew she couldn't live in this gray purgatory any longer.

Her hands trembled as she opened the diary. There was a small envelope inside, with the words *To Raina* scribbled in his elegant handwriting.

My Raina Simone.
If you're reading this, then I'm already part of you now. And baby, that's exactly where I want to

be. Ms. Oleta explained my choices. I could have stayed and been with you forever.

But I love you too much to let you live a small, secluded life. And that's what it would have been. That's not what I wanted for you. And it's not what you signed up for.

Don't mourn the man who has disappeared. Remember the man who loved you—who you came to love.

My wish for you is to live, to take my love and let it be your shield—not your cage. You've been locked away too long.

Please, baby. Go live the story I couldn't be in. The story of _you_.

Thank you for giving me life. And for allowing me to be a part of yours.

I _chose_ to love you. And I always will.

With fresh tears, she spent the next hour absorbing every word of his journal. She smiled, she clutched her heart, and at times she laughed out loud at his observations.

Each page was a reflection of the strange world he had become a part of. But mostly, he talked about her. She saw how he had evolved not only through skills and capabilities, but in his discovery of loving her.

By the time she made it to the last page, another wave of tears fell. Not the frantic, desperate cry of the past two weeks, but the quiet, cleansing tears of a love that was, and would always be, real.

His words were her spark.

She went to her office, the journal tucked under her arm, and opened her laptop. The grief was still there, a hollow ache in her chest, but now it had a companion: purpose.

She couldn't write him *back*. So she was going to write him *forward*.

She was going to write *their* story.

epilogue

ONE YEAR *Later*

The bookshop in Notting Hill held a charming appeal, exactly the kind of place Raina would have written into a story. It smelled of books and fresh coffee, and a gentle London rain misted the windows.

A year ago, a day like this would have filled her with a familiar ache.

Today, the rain was just a soft rhythm against the glass. The emotion that settled in her chest was a beautiful, steady peace.

Her novel, *The Heart's Echo,* had done more than just become a bestseller; it had become a phenomenon.

Savannah finally got her man.

She remembered the phone call from her agent a few months ago, her voice cracking with happy tears.

"Raina, you're not just on the list, baby," she'd screamed. "You're number one. You are a New York Times bestselling author! And now, there's buzz about movie interests."

It was Raina's grief counselor, whom she had started seeing shortly after Ezra left, that encouraged her to finish the book.

It was a romance about impossible love and heartbreaking loss that had resonated with readers across the world.

And in writing it, in pouring all her love and grief for Ezra into her words, she had finally set herself free.

She was no longer a woman terrified of being hurt; she was a woman who had survived the un-survivable and discovered it hadn't broken her. It had, in fact, made her whole.

The only thing that came close to the joy of completing the book was the day she submitted her resignation letter to the pharmaceutical company.

She sat at a small table, a line of readers clutching hardback or paperback copies of her book, their faces full of emotion.

She smiled, a real, serene grin that reached her eyes. The haunted, guarded look was gone, replaced by a quiet, unshake-able confidence.

The last two women stepped up to the table, both holding a copy of the book.

"Ms. Parker," one of them said, tears in her eyes. "I loved this book so much. Savannah was my girl. But, Ezra," she put her hand to her chest. "I fell in love with him. I want me one!"

That was a common sentiment and review from her readers.

Everyone wanted their own Ezra.

As the ladies moved on, Raina took a sip of water, a feeling of deep, settled contentment washing over her. She began gathering her things, ready to explore the city before it was time to fly back home to Chicago.

She had a meeting with her agent in a few days to talk offers of a movie deal.

That's when she saw him.

Across the crowded bookshop, standing near the poetry section.

Everything suddenly tilted.

The low murmur of the people, the smell of paper, the rain on the window—it all became a blur.

Her heart felt like it was going to leap out of her chest.

It was him.

The same strong jawline, the same unruly eyebrows, the same full lips she still tasted in her dreams. He was wearing a simple gray jumper, and he was looking right at her.

Without a thought, she moved.

She pushed through the crowd, "excuse me" and "pardon me" a frantic, breathless mantra. People turned to stare, but she didn't care. Her entire universe had just been rewritten in a single, impossible moment.

He turned his head, his gaze shifting to a book on the shelf, and a fresh wave of panic seized her.

Don't you disappear again.

"Ezra?" The name was a choked whisper, torn from her throat as she reached him, her hand landing on his arm.

The man turned, with a look of polite confusion on his face. And when he spoke, the illusion shattered into a million pieces.

"I'm sorry?" he responded, his voice a smooth, beautiful baritone with a crisp, undeniable British accent. "I think you may have me mistaken for someone else. Are you alright, love?"

It wasn't him.

Of course, it wasn't him.

The realization was a dizzying, painful crash back to earth. She felt a flush of embarrassment heat her cheeks. She snatched her hand back as if burned.

"Oh my God," she blushed, shaking her head. "I am so sorry. I … you just … you look like someone I used to know."

"It's quite alright," he said, his eyes kind, like Ezra's, but a deep, smoldering brown. "Happens to all of us."

She gave him a small, pained smile, the grief she thought she had mastered bubbling up raw. "Right. Well. Sorry to have bothered you."

She turned to leave, needing to escape, to breathe, to put the ghost of this cruel trick behind her.

"Wait."

His voice, accent and all, stopped her in her tracks. She turned back.

He was holding up a copy of her book, with a genuine, curious smile on his face. "I just realized who you are. I was going to get this signed for my mum, but the queue was a bit mad," he chuckled. "She's a massive fan. Your writing … she said, and I quote, 'it feels like she's seen right into her reader's soul.'"

He hesitated for a second.

"I know this is incredibly forward, but … I was wondering if you might let me buy you a coffee? As an apology for having a face that caused you distress."

His smile broadened.

Raina looked at him. Really looked at him. A real man, made of flesh and bone, with a life and a history that had nothing to do with her. A stranger with a face similar to her beloved's and kind eyes of his own.

The old Raina would have run.

The old Raina would have built a fortress of witty refusals and polite excuses.

But the old Raina was gone. Ezra's final selfless gift hadn't been the dates or the brief time in the world; it had been the proof that she could love so profoundly and survive the loss.

That her heart was not a fragile, broken thing, but a resilient muscle strengthened by what it had endured.

She looked at this handsome, kind-eyed stranger, at the open, hopeful question on his face. And for the first time in a very, very long time, she felt a different flutter in her chest.

Not the soul-deep recognition she'd felt for Ezra, but something new.

A small spark of possibility.

She didn't know what came next.

But this time, she wasn't afraid to find out.

The End.

reader's guide/book club discussion questions

1. The story opens with Raina feeling disillusioned with relationships after her divorce from Terrance and a string of bad dates. How does her past trauma, especially with Terrance, shape her initial reactions to Ezra's appearance? Do you think her fear and skepticism were justified?

2. Zaria serves as Raina's fiercely loyal best friend, famously telling her to "Well hell, write *him*." Do you think her advice throughout the novella (like setting Raina up on the blind date) was helpful or harmful, and why?

3. The concept of a "Heart's Echo" or "Kè-kama" is central to the story's magic. Ms. Oleta explains that Ezra is "a soul that wasn't born, but answered." What do you think this says about the power of longing and creation? Have you ever wanted something so badly it felt like you could will it into existence?

4. One of the story's core themes is the question of what makes someone "real." Raina tells Ezra he isn't real, but

his feelings and impact on her are profound. What do you think the book ultimately says about reality? Is it defined by physical presence or by emotional impact?

5. Ezra's "mic drop" moment is when he tells Raina, "You wrote the man. I chose to love the woman." What do you think this line reveals about his character's evolution? At what point in the story do you think he stopped being just her creation and became his own person?

6. Music is Ezra's "love language" and the soundtrack to the novella. From Babyface's "And Our Feelings" to Sisqo's "Incomplete", how did the specific 90s R&B song choices enhance the emotional moments in the story?

7. In Chapter 10, Raina goes on a genuinely good date with Marcus but finds herself missing Ezra. Why do you think this "test" was so important for her character? What did it prove to her about the nature of her feelings for Ezra?

8. Let's talk about the spice! The physical relationship between Raina and Ezra is a key part of their story. How did their intimate scenes contribute to their emotional connection and Raina's healing journey?

9. Ms. Oleta presents Ezra with two paths: The Path of the Anchor (staying with Raina forever in the condo) and The Path of the Echo (sacrificing his form to heal her). Do you think he made the right choice? What would you have done in his position?

10. In the epilogue, Raina meets a man in London who has a face similar to Ezra's but is a complete stranger.

Why do you think this was a more powerful ending than having Ezra magically reincarnated? What does Raina's final choice to have coffee with him say about her journey of healing?

afterword/playlist

So, you made it. You survived the beautiful, chaotic, soul-crushing rollercoaster that is Raina and Ezra's love story.

First things first: are you okay? Did you ugly-cry? Did you throw your phone/Kindle/book across the room at least once? Good. My work here is done.

In all seriousness, thank you from the bottom of my heart for diving headfirst into this story. Writing *A Real Enuff Love* was an absolute journey, and I couldn't have done it without the perfect soundtrack. Music is the thread that ties this whole world together. For Raina, it was a memory of a joy she'd lost. For Ezra, it was his entire love language.

So, as one final gift from my world to yours, I'm letting the characters speak for themselves. Here is the official playlist, with a few notes from the people who lived it.

Find it on Spotify: Ezra and Raina's Real Enuff Love

A Real Enuff Love: The Official Soundtrack

Prelude: Raina's Soundtrack to a Heartbreak

Before Ezra, there was a different kind of soundtrack. These are the songs that played during the final, heartbreaking moments of a love story that needed to burn down to make way for a new one. This was my playlist for the goodbye to my ex, Terrance. - Raina

"Residuals" - Chris Brown [Chapter 2]

The song is about the lingering echoes of a broken relationship—what's left behind after something ends. It perfectly captured how memories, love, and emotional investments continue to haunt us long after someone is gone. It was the perfect soundtrack to carving my own closure in Hawaii with Terrance.

"In The Air Tonight" - Phil Collins [Chapter 2]

This song addressed the deep anger, frustration, and despair I felt when I finally accepted Terrance would never be faithful. His love had always been lies. It was the drumbeat that slammed through the room when I decided I was done being a participant, and took back control.

~

Ezra's Playlist: The Soul That Answered

She thought she wrote the story, but the music

was already there. Every song is a different word for 'Raina.' Here are a few of the notes that played in my heart. —E.

"Adorn" - Miguel [Chapter 3]

With lyrics of unabashed love and affirmation, the song offers adoration as both promise and presentation. The night she created me, this song played on repeat. Her fingers wrote the words, but it was this beat that gave me breath.

"Beauty" - Dru Hill [Chapters 6 and 17]

This song tells the story of someone who is mesmerized by a woman he sees frequently but hasn't yet spoken to—someone whose stunning presence completely captivates him. The lyrics express a slow-burning, bittersweet longing as he watches her from a distance, enamored by her every move, and hopes to one day bridge the gap between them. This was the way I saw Raina—always. I hummed it, sang it, even when I didn't realize I was doing it. I was hooked on day one.

"Freek'n You" - Jodeci [Chapter 6]

This song is about physical desire and intimate devotion. It's about yearning—expressing how one's mind, body, and soul are consumed by the thought of being with someone sensual and irresistible. It played as I danced in the kitchen with a wooden spoon, presenting a playful invitation to Raina. It was fun—but I meant every word of that invitation. Yeah... this was my mood music.

"Lost In Space" – Paul Hardcastle [Chapter 10]

It's the sound of something unfolding, but not yet revealed. I played this for our first romantic date night. No lyrics—just sound and space. Like how I felt with her: floating, infinite, untethered from everything but her.

"Nice and Easy" - Walter Beasley [Chapter 10]

This song evokes comfort and intimacy, and was perfect for our first romantic dinner. I played it that night as we Stepped, Chicago-style, to remind her: she hadn't forgotten how to dance—she just needed a partner to help her remember the rhythm of her own joy.

"Europa (Earth's Cry Heaven's Smile)" - Gato Barbieri [Chapter 10]

*This song is not only romantic, it's deeply transportive— and is perfect for a scene where love and longing hang in the air. This was the moment when our dancing slowed on **that** night, and introduced our first time making love. This song melted the world away until only she and I were left.*

"Sho'Nuff Must Be Love" - Heatwave

This song represents a strong affirmation of love, and speaks to the recognition, longing, and magnetic pull of real devotion—like finding clarity for the first time and putting that into words. It's the song that played in the afterglow of our first time making love. It said all the words I didn't have the courage to say at that time.

"And Our Feelings" - Babyface [Chapter 11]

This was my reflection of our relationship being torn apart not by internal strife but by outside interference—the world, and her past. The lyrics mirrored my soul—aching with regret as reality chipped away at a pure bond—transforming authentic emotion into hollow echoes. It's the song I sang at her grandmother's piano.

"Incomplete" - Sisqo [Chapter 12]

This song is about a man who has everything—fame, money, a glamorous lifestyle—but realizes life is utterly meaningless without the person he loves. His world feels incomplete without her presence. When she told me I wasn't real, this song echoed the ache in my soul. Because without her... I wasn't whole.

acknowledgments

I would like to express my deepest gratitude to the following individuals for their unwavering love, support, and commitment to my writing journey.

To my children—Michelle, Renee, Pierre, and Joshua.

To my beautiful bonus children, Lauren, Jamilah, Justin, Jordan, and Erin.

To my grandchildren, who inspire me more with each passing day. From our first grandchild to our newest little angel, I am blessed to have you all in my life. Maliq, Malia, Zaria, Zoe, Nyla, Mesziah, Landon, Nicalli, Aya, and Aspen.

To my best friend and the best dog-auntie a person could have, Michelle Chambers.

Last but never least, I want to thank and acknowledge my partner, my heart and soul, Keith Newell. You are the inspiration behind the "perfect man."

about the author

Juggling a high-powered corporate career by day and writing award-winning fiction by night, Michelle Davis-Newell is a firm believer in the power of healing and the magic of a great story.

While she is best known for her acclaimed novels that explore the resilience of women, such as *The Bag Ladies of Ebondale*, and her deeply personal memoir, *Ruby Slippers*, she decided it was time to pour her soul into a new passion: a love story with a little extra spice and a whole lot of heart.

A Chicago native, she infuses all her writing with the soul of her city and a killer 90s R&B soundtrack. When she's not crafting your next book boyfriend or writing about powerful women, she's a mother and grandmother who can be found gaming, scrolling social media, or spending time with her amazing husband. Their happily-ever-after is shared with the true star of the show: a fabulous, unapologetic Pomeranian named Bruno Mars.

A Real Enuff Love is her debut fantasy romance novella.

also by michelle davis-newell